volume 1 spring 2002

TRUTH x 24

Short Fiction by Writers
From the Hudson Valley, New York

✷

Edited by Brent Robison

Bliss Plot
PRESS

Prima Materia
Volume 1, Spring 2002

Acknowledgment:
"Linguistics" by Jennie Litt originally appeared in COLUMBIA: A JOURNAL OF LITERATURE AND ART, in a somewhat different form.

Published by Bliss Plot Press, PO Box 68, Mt. Tremper, NY 12457
Editor/Publisher: Brent Robison
Associate Publisher: Wendy Klein

For subscription information, inquire at the address above or by e-mail at primamateria@brentrobison.com.

Submissions: Unsolicited manuscripts should include a self-addressed, stamped envelope (SASE) or an e-mail address; otherwise we cannot respond. For submission guidelines, send an SASE with your request, or visit www.brentrobison.com/primamateria.htm.

ISSN 0-9718908-0-3
ISBN 1538-9553

Printed in the United States of America

Cover design by Brent Robison
Photo: "World" © Brent Robison, 1997

Dedicated to Cal:
twenty years gone, never forgotten

The Hudson River Valley

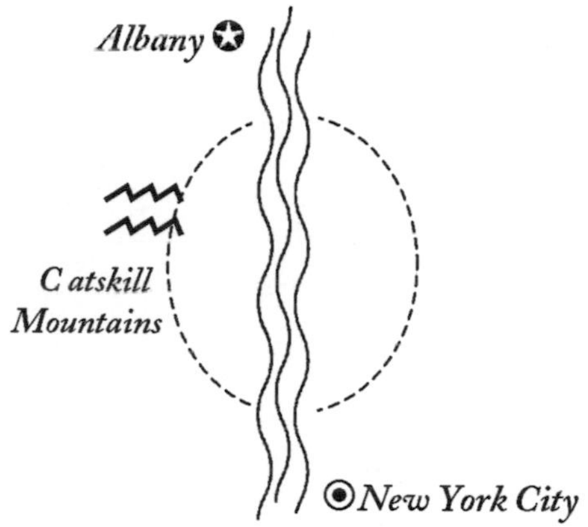

In 1609, Henry Hudson sailed the Half Moon up the river that would one day bear his name. He called it the River of Mountains and wrote of its valley, "It is as pleasant a land as one can tread upon." Washington Irving later made local folk tales famous with "The Legend of Sleepy Hollow" and "Rip Van Winkle," capturing a dark magic that most certainly hides in these hills. A surprising number of arts colonies and spiritual retreats have found refuge in these wooded valleys for over a century. Today, rumor has it that the region claims more "artists" per capita than any comparable area in the country. And UFOs as well.

With "The City," the center of the world, just an easy jaunt downriver, and world-class culture swarming north to our doorstep, we can still enjoy the sight of a black bear eating berries in the backyard. There's something in the air here, or the soil, or the water. There's an energy in the Hudson Valley that has called creative spirits from all over the world. There's serious talent here, working in secret in these woods and river towns. This book gives a sampling of the stories we have to tell.

Prima Materia

Volume 1 Spring 2002

Contents

To find the philosopher's stone:
"Pray, read, read, read, read again, labor, and discover."

—*Mutus Liber*
(Wordless Book)
1677

Introduction

Welcome to the first issue of ***Prima Materia***. Here are twenty-four pieces of writing, diverse in theme, style, and length, but all written by authors to whom this place, the Hudson Valley, is home. This is a good place to be.

Right now, the forest is dark outside my windows. I'm sitting in a soft chair with warm lamplight falling on the keyboard and classic jazz on the stereo, low, not quite drowning out the sleety rain pelting the skylight over my head. The house is filled with the aroma of brown rice and homemade vegetable soup. The fire in the woodstove pops and cracks. I am happy to be writing this.

Prima Materia was born of a tribal urge: my desire to connect with fiction writers, to find them wherever they may be hiding in the woods and small towns of this valley, of these mountains. To give them a chance to be seen and heard. Local poets seem everywhere visible and audible, memoirists only a little less so, but I needed to search out those who labor over dense manuscripts carefully as blind men, finding deep truth in a volatile mixture of imagination and memory that can only be controlled, when fortune smiles, by craft. The two dozen writers in these pages are brave, skilled, keen of ear, and open of heart. I am proud to give them voice, and to make the claim: *Truth x 24*.

A meaningful coincidence for me is that ***Prima Materia*** officially entered the world on September 11, 2001. I was on the phone with the newspaper, placing my first call for submissions, when I began to hear the buzz in the office: something had happened at the World Trade Center. Precisely what effect that event plus the ensuing madness have had on this, the actual volume, is impossible to say, except that everything slowed down. It became important to me that our debut *not* be a reflexive response to this singular tragedy, and the authors who sent their work seemed to agree. Maybe in some future issue, we will give considered exploration to our new post-9/11 reality; maybe not. This adventure is creating itself.

A fond, if unrealistic, wish of mine is that you will read these stories in the order I've presented them. I hope that you'll go on a journey with us, a bus ride through lives much like, and much unlike, your own. There are delicate threads that weave through these pieces, making of them a single big story. Read with an eye for the subtle, and you'll see the strands. But more important: if the unity of spirit here resonates more deeply in you than any surface textures might suggest, then our newborn publishing venture is already a success.

Walking the editor's road has given me a few interesting discoveries. First, as this volume began to come together, several voices seemed to blend into one. A chorus arose out of the chatter. It is the voice of a young woman out on her own, making her way in a difficult world. Maybe she rides alone on a bus through an unwelcoming city; maybe she struggles with beauty or love; maybe she's a child or a mother or a wife. Maybe she even surrounds, gives context to, the masculine in these stories. There are courage and humor, honesty and gentleness; there is a bittersweet wisdom in this chorus of harmonizing voices. This is music the world needs to hear.

Another encounter along the path was with the foggy valley that separates fiction from memoir. I am in love with the alchemy that fuses the "real" with the "unreal," memory spiked like punch with unruly imagination, a steaming brew under whose influence Scribe is transformed into Creator, and a world is born: something out of nothing. It's not enough that a story is "true;" the wildest kind of fabrication may be far more True. But fantastic imagining (sometimes called "creativity") is no guarantee of merit either. The ineffable presence of the Artist makes the difference: technique and content find a balance. Or maybe each lone reader is the only judge of whether a work has the "ring of truth." It's a mystery, this mix. And mystery is what I like.

It's no mystery that good fiction demands compelling characters. Compelling ("real") characters are created in clear-minded empathy, in going deep inside, using the uniquely human power of imagination to see through other eyes, to "walk a mile in another's shoes." To write fiction from the heart is to love your fellow beings, warts and all; to know, as Ginsberg told us, that all are holy. And to read it is to partake of that spirit. Literature need not be full of "message" to be of first importance; if it has an empathic soul, we need it desperately. This venture we are undertaking together is not trivial; it is one more candle in a midnight cave.

One last thought: I don't mind that many of the pieces here would never qualify, by textbook definition, as a "story." They feel like fragments of something much larger, which the best fiction always does, no matter its form. These may look like everyday scenes from contemporary life, but actually they are scraps of parchment from ancient seabeds, diamonds both polished and rough, gold made from lead. I hope you'll agree with me that, here in our lovely green and watery nook of the planet, we should be grateful. All around us, our neighbors are quietly making good work, molding new worlds from the right stuff, the essential substance, the *prima materia*. Please, enjoy.

—Brent Robison
March 2002
Mt. Tremper, NY

TRUTH x 24

Kate Schapira

All Saints

More leaves are off the trees than on; leaves swirl around me on my way to the bus stop. For home visits I try not to dress too nicely, but the wind sneaks into me wherever it can, the more so because it is already getting dark and the trick-or-treaters are assembling on their front porches. Parents make concessions of witches' hats or face paint, harry their children and their neighbors' into some semblance of a herd. Tutus, plastic pumpkin baskets, monster masks, reflective tape.

Nine years ago on Halloween, while driving home, I hit a four-year-old girl with my Toyota Camry, crushing both of her legs. She was the last in a line of trick-or-treaters. I thought all of them had made it across; I had even left a few seconds for stragglers before stepping on the gas. At first I thought I had hit a dog. I stopped, thinking I would take it to the vet. Her legs were under my front wheel. Her head was bleeding. I screamed almost in unison with the grown-up-in-charge, a woman named Anne Carmel who testified in my favor, explaining how I had stopped immediately, called 911 myself on my car phone, offered to take the girl to the hospital and pay all her fees. That last turned out not to be necessary. Emily Kwan died in intensive care, her legs mixed up with her tutu. When I was in prison I would think of it like that and start giggling wetly, so that I had to kneel down and press the teeth of my comb into the back of my neck. She visited me in no other way. Fortunately—I say this advisedly—her head had hit the pavement with enough force that she never regained consciousness.

The bus driver says, "How's it goin'?" Willa is a saint. She drives this route on Tuesdays, Thursdays, and Sundays, determined to support her kids without any help from their crack-dealing dad. I would prefer silence. I'm tired from my day—one of the kids simply failed to turn up, and I think Doreen may be drinking again—but I say, "Not too bad, Willa. You?"

"Ismail cut his first tooth. I saw it peekin' when I left for work and he wouldn't shut up cryin'." Pride makes her seem less tired, the creases in her uniform sharper, like Ismail pushed out that tooth by sheer force of will.

"You tell him congratulations for me and give him an extra kiss." She opens the door for me. She says, "You gonna be cold."

"My place isn't far." A couple of blocks. I wave to her once the door is closed. She waves back from her small dirty envelope of warmth and light. I'm thirty-eight, almost twice her age, and our lives only knock elbows on the bus from town, but she's probably my closest friend here in upstate New York. I did three years for involuntary manslaughter. I started on my MSW in Albion and finished it at SUNY Oneonta after I got out. I live and work not twenty minutes from the campus in a small town with few jobs. Towns like that always have something for social workers to do.

The leaves skitter, get caught in circular eddies that take them a foot or so into the air, then collapse. Porch lights are on. My neighbors have bagged their leaves in plastic pumpkins and ghosts, hung fake cobwebs from their porches, stuffed and propped up scarecrows. These three blocks, mine and the next two over, mostly house youngish families with kids younger than high school. For many of them it's the first house they've owned. There's a light, ashy salting of Oneonta kids and single people like me who never put out candy.

Leslie, my downstairs neighbor, is in her doorway adjusting some kind of glowing hanging decoration or accessory.

She doesn't know I've been inside, and isn't too clear on what I do now since confidentiality is vital to my work. I, on the other hand, was treated to a blow-by-blow account, literally, of Leslie's odyssey. First she was a battered daughter. Then she was a battered wife and abusive mother. Then she lost her sons to the state and started drinking herself into a persistent vegetative state. She goes to AA now, rotund and game; she always sponsors new arrivals. Her kids are seven and nine. She sees them once a month in the presence of their adoptive parents. She says they forgive her.

I've never been an addict, a joiner, or a flagellant. I'm not one to stand up and testify. They didn't know what to do with me in prison. Leslie is sort of like Eeyore on uppers, but sometimes the company is nice. We drink hot chocolate together, Swiss Miss with the tiny marshmallows right in it, the way some people meet for a beer. Even in summer.

Leslie calls, "Hey! Come check this out." I go over obediently, swinging my canvas bag of files against my thigh. The thing in the doorway is a pale plastic doodad with a ghost's face. She says gleefully, "Give it a tap."

I reach up and tap the object lightly. It emits squeals and snorts and what I presume is meant to be a high-pitched laugh. Leslie giggles with it. "Isn't it something? You should've seen your face!" I hadn't known my face was doing anything. She frowns. "You think the kids will go for it?"

"Sure," I say with confidence. "They'll get a big kick out of it."

"Oh good," she says, "that's why I got it." We lapse into silence. Leslie has bouts of talkativeness but they dry up as quickly as they come on, and all the small talk has been bleached out of me. I've never talked about the big things, only thought about them in the car. Before I killed Emily I was a sales rep for a publishing house. I wore heels and earrings and got my hair done every two months.

In Albion I worked in the laundry, the kitchens, down in the boiler room. I pled guilty at my arraignment and had my sister

Elaine, who is Born Again and no longer speaks to me, sell the Camry I would never drive again. It seemed like the perfect punishment: being kept off the road. I had to work hard to get them to take away something I really cared about.

My first car was a crumpled white Honda hatchback that Elaine had wrecked twice. I've always had a body like a burden: heavy-hipped, slump-shouldered, thick glasses, thicker neck. In gym class I was slow, on the dance floor I was fat. But by turning a key I could own a body, fast, responsive, even sleek in its way. My own body was something to haul around. My real skin was metal and glass, my real muscles pistons and sparks. I might eat Sno-Balls, slug coffee, lie around for hours, but I loved that solid, ordinary Camry till it hummed. The best part of the job was driving in between the dreary, ceiling-lit stores, even on the parkway sometimes, windows open, speed in my hair. That was the difference between a dull body and a dull car.

Leslie and the other tenants parked in our building's cracked lot with its unexplainable pink spot, a filled-in circle ten steps in diameter. Leslie's Corolla was ghost outlined in the greenish backdoor light, ghost of my old car come to haunt me as Emily Kwan had never come. One woman in my cube dreamed every few nights about the son she beat to death, traded cigarettes and food for No-Doz so she wouldn't have to sleep. Most of the women there weren't nearly so dramatic, doing five-to-twelve for drug offenses, some in for their second or third bid. Leslie doesn't know I've been in prison. No one here does, only a couple secretaries at Oneonta who had to be told so they could give me credit for my work there. Nice women, shaped a little like me, but softer and spreading from years of desk jobs, and with higher hair.

Leslie follows me around to the back lot. "You'd never know it had anything wrong with it," she sighs. "I wish cars showed on the outside how many problems they have on the inside. Cars and people," she amends. "Then you'd know what you were dealing with at least." I nod to show I'm listening. Leslie never got out of that adolescent stage where they're the only one who's ever figured something out. Everything original. "It sounded fine on the way home," she goes on, "got up to fifty with no problems. I give it a month, tops, before something else goes wrong."

Up to fifty with no problems.... Sounds approach us on the wind, the progress of an undersized tribe and their distracted parents. Witches and pirates, Little Mermaids and Aladdins. Because of the clouds, the moon looks like it's scooting, the wind makes itself heard in the high branches, moving fast, fast....

"Leslie," I say, hardly able to talk around my own audacity, "you know what, maybe I will get some candy to put out. Is the CVS still open?"

"Till nine. But you're not gonna walk there?" Her concern is real but I have no room for it. "Well, no," I say, "I was wondering if I could borrow the car—I'll be very careful, I promise." And easily, "I'm a good driver—" I let it hang although this is the one thing in the world I'm certain of.

"Sure! Of course you can. I didn't know you could drive at all or I'd 've offered. There's gas in it and everything."

"Thanks, Leslie, you're a saint." When did I last say that? High school? "Is there anything you need, anything I can get for you while I'm out?"

"Nope," she says after a second of earnest, eye-rolling thought, as if her shopping list is printed under her eyebrows. "Wait, yeah, there is." She digs into her pocket. "Shit. I'll be back in a sec, I just have to run in and get some change, and I'll get you the keys too." I wait for her, my blood flowing harshly, the hairs on my arms about to take off. She drops crumpled singles into my hand. "Marlboro Lights if they have them; otherwise, anything but menthol. And here's the key." It still has the greasy garage tag on it, as well as house keys and a plastic plaque that reads, "Everyone's entitled to be stupid but you're abusing the privilege." I say, "I really appreciate this, Leslie," and she says, "No problem. Just bring it back in one piece," the way you say something you know you don't have to worry about. I wait another minute, watch her light go on. Lighted windows from outside at night have made me wordlessly sad since I was a kid.

I get a static shock from the door handle as I lift it. The driver's seat feels right in a way that bus seats, train seats, even the passenger side never do. I remember high school dances, boys with men's hands bending to press close the asses of the lucky girls. The driver's seat curves around me as my hands curve around the wheel. I turn the key. I press the gas.

Panic. I don't know how to drive to the CVS, *Oh God what am I doing*, my headlights outline two fairy princesses holding their father's hands. I turn a corner without any real idea where I am, like it hasn't been me finding her way around these last three years. I hit the main road and head for the lights of town, too jittery and numb to feel the car around me. Keep a terrified mile under the speed limit, pray the taillight that was broken a month ago works now. I pull shaking into the CVS parking lot. The skinny permed girl who sells me the cigarettes must think I need a nicotine fix. I also buy a bag of peanut butter cups and one of Almond Joys.

Candy was worth more than cigarettes. You could buy cigarettes with your five cents an hour. Candy was basically contraband. You could trade cigarettes for it. Once I got hold of some in return for a favor and gorged myself. A prison bathroom is no place to get diarrhea. I felt slightly nauseated looking at the bags. So many of the women put on huge amounts of weight in prison. I pitied them and looked down on them as much as I looked down on the women who spent hours on their hair. One woman had been a hairdresser on the outside but there was only so much she could do without her chemicals and combs. Even so her services were in high demand despite her constant farting. She was one of the fat ones. I couldn't understand adding to the bag of crap you had to haul around through all that concrete.

I realize that I've made the left toward home out of the parking lot: already my instincts are taking over. The transplant has been successful. Soon I feel fine about picking up speed and taking one hand off the wheel to unwrap and eat a peanut butter cup. I roll the window down and wish I hadn't eaten the chocolate;

it greases the smell of the night air. *I don't want to let this go* becomes *Why should I let this go?* becomes *I can't let this go.*

Instead of turning onto my street, I stay on the main road till the houses dwindle and with them the threat of small, glittery, shadowy people, dashing out into the road, too young to look both ways. I take a minute to feel guilty about Leslie and her good nature: this is the first intentional advantage I've ever taken, if you don't count all the sales talk. Then I was lost with the motion of the car, rocking slightly around the big loose curves of the county road, headlights sweeping toward me, past me, and taillights vanishing in the depths of the rear-view mirror.

I was scrupulous, at the hearing, to not take advantage. It wasn't hard. I had a degree in Sales and Marketing; the Kwans were both professionals, he a science teacher, she a doctor. But I didn't hire a lawyer, I didn't try to defend myself, I even maneuvered them into taking my true freedom away. I was a good person; I'd always been a good person. Anybody could see I felt bad. Anybody could see I was taking responsibility, that I wasn't a danger to society. Prison was a gesture. A nod to the Kwans, a way of saying yes, I understand.

I haven't thought of it this clearly before, of course. I had said, "You don't get to feel sorry for yourself," and you don't get to drive and you don't get to think straight. I concerned myself with being a good person: Sandy at the office would come in, "Oh god, you guys, can anyone take the Houstons this week? Anyone? My mom's gall bladder is acting up again, she needs someone to stay with her, but they shouldn't go two weeks without a visit. I feel terrible even asking." And I would say, "I think I can do it."

"Oh, Ronnie, you're a saint. Here's the file. Call me tonight, you know, if you have any questions before I leave."

I tell myself I'm not trying to do penance and the people who might say, "You're kidding yourself," I have eliminated from my life. A choice comes up in front of me: County Route 71 North? Or South? I make a left. People are very casual about sainthood. I don't pretend I do very much for my kids, their mothers, their own kids, their foster families. I don't bleed for them. Isn't that what being a saint is about?

I am in my true body after nine years in slumping flesh and my true body may leak but it doesn't bleed. The dim suggestion of cliffs on either side of me gives way to fields. Night driving is the best, stripped down. There's no scenery, no colorful foliage, no majestic vistas or microcosms. At most the dark divides into moonlight, starlight, streetlight, headlight. Few people are out. Those with families anyway are home by now, picking through their stashes. Trading two Hershey Kisses for a Baby Ruth. I unwrap another peanut butter cup, blind and precise as Braille. I could no more teach someone how to drive than teach them how to walk.

What I don't know is what I owe the dead. And the dead can't tell me because she didn't live all that long; why should I believe her? Leslie might have called the cops by now, not because she thinks I've done anything illegal but because she thinks something illegal might have happened to me. It would be like her to worry. Maybe I'm dead in a ditch, "for all I know," she'd say. What was a gesture for me is legal fact for the state of New York. If I am caught I will be arrested. If I make it across the state line that state will extradite me. They're much clearer about this than I am.

I've stopped keeping track of my rights and lefts. The peanut butter cups are more than half gone; I have to grope around in the bag. I suppose I could just keep driving. I say out loud, "Emily," feeling stupid. Tonight would be the night, of all nights, that she would speak, that the border would thin. I hear the slight stutter of the engine. My own breathing if I concentrate. All the little hypochondriac murmurs you hear in any vehicle. I never heard Emily's actual voice, just the screams in her wake, and maybe that's part of it. Voices are hard to hear at the best of times.

The air is paler and, if possible, chillier. I pull off the road into a dirt driveway, up onto a wet grass bank. I turn the car off to let it rest and open the bag of Almond Joys. On second thought I get out and climb up on the warm hood, which bounces a little under me. Birds are singing. Warmth soaks upward; I lie back against the windshield. I will sit here till the cops come with their questions and the saints with their forgiveness, of which I want no part.

Philip Pardi

Seven Postcards

#1

Sitting here, opposite you, your latte keeps you busy as I write what I'll send you from the mailbox out front the minute you're gone. When you read this, remember: you lent me this pen and I kept it.

#2

We talk, talk of things. Each thing its own trajectory, you say, corks pop, plates spin, spirits seduce. I'd like to be seduced, I say. What I meant was: left to myself I chase each shaky certainty to no end but to begin again, and some things are best when unbegun.

#3

Do you remember, as you read this, the way sirens came near, so loud we stopped talking, and you looked out the window, hoping for a glimpse? For a moment, every piece of glass in this place reflected red in an echo that haloed all around you, and I can't help but think sirens become you.

#4

What I meant was: what is is without you, a calm and clement chaos, folding palm into fist, forcing fist into palm, and ours is not ours at all. I meant: each thing we see we steal, then steel ourselves for what must pass here, where longing led us, left us.

#5

So many, so many that none now appear. No signs of life, no signs of death, no ghosts, even, just the conviction they've been here and gone, left us noteless and guessing.

#6

Seven identical armadillos. What's a postcard with no armadillo? You ask me what I'm writing, and I say: armadillo postcards. To someone I knew only briefly.

#7

I've just watched you walk away. In fact, I can still see you, waiting to cross 14th street. You're looking up, thinking: it's going to rain. The waiter just cleared away your mug. It's getting dark. Soon it'll be time to leave. The city won't notice you're gone.

Jennie Litt

✷

Linguistics

A man and a woman lived in a provincial city over which a layer of clouds, swollen with emanations from the reeking lake and factory chimneys, hung heavy and unmoving.

The man and woman spent many hours discussing Epic theatre, the Bauhaus, early creation myths, word derivations, and Platonic forms.

When they had used a word, they would discard it onto the pile of used words at their feet. At first, the woman conscientiously swept all the used words into a dustpan and threw them away every night. But as months passed she swept less often, and carelessly. Words built up in corners and under the bed; a fine layer sprinkled the wooden floor. The woman and man had to brush discarded words from the soles of their feet before putting on their socks.

The words continued to build up. Now when they opened the apartment door, words spilled into the stairwell. They each kept one pair of word-encrusted shoes on a high shelf for daily use; their other shoes were buried under a drift of words. They stumbled and slid on the words like people who try to run on fine sand.

The apartment took on the aspect of a beach. The woman and man built word-castles under the hot blue ceiling. The potted palm grew fronds like giant wings, and bore coconuts. Gulls scavenged in the dunes. Distantly, the woman and man could hear the hiss of surf. It seemed to come from no particular direction and from all directions at once. Listening for it, the woman and man walked for a night and a day until they found a hissing steam radiator half-buried in the sand.

They were hot and tired, so they rested in the sand by the radiator. They were thirsty, but had nothing to drink. They talked of water in parched voices for an hour, and their words built up around them until all that could be seen of the radiator was the curve of one silver pipe. Beyond it, the short grasses appeared wavy through the radiating steam.

It occurred to them that if they smashed the pipe, they might each catch a mouthful or two of hot vapor. They would have preferred coconut milk, but the coconut palm was far away, where the path of their footprints originated. The man had a hammer in his pocket and the woman had a rock. They beat on the exposed pipe with hammer and rock until it rang like a bell. They beat harder, perspiring. The pipe rang more and more loudly.

The song of the ringing pipe traveled up their arms and vibrated in their chests. It resonated in their abdomens, knees, and feet. It filled their heads and flowed out of their mouths. The song in their mouths left no room for words. When they could beat on the pipe no longer, they found they could not stop singing. They sang as they exhaled and sang as they inhaled. Helplessly, they sang and sang. All of a sudden, the pipe cracked in two, releasing a spurt of water that hissed and steamed as it struck the hot sand.

The water spread like a dark stain across the sand. It filled the hollows of their footprints, and the sand-angels they had made when they had lain down to rest. The little pools overflowed and trickled into one another. The hillock of sand on which the man and woman stood quickly became an island. A golden archipelago of sand hillocks disappeared beneath the rising water. The man and woman waded in water to their ankles. The water rose around them. They felt the sand give way to water beneath their feet. They rose with the rising water.

Neither was a very good swimmer. They clung to each other, treading water with their free hand, their eyes and mouths closed against oncoming waves. They drifted for a while in a blind panic until they felt something tickling their feet and legs. Terrified, they opened their eyes.

Through the clear, greenish water, they saw a lacy network of darker green swaying gently below them in the mild current. Something darted through it, a thin diamond shape with a bulbous eye. They rested against a hard gray surface. The man moved his hand and saw he had torn something away: a flattish slate-colored egg that opened to reveal a small, pulsing, mouth-shaped creature between two opaline walls.

In that world of water, they forgot they had ever known the words "seaweed," "fish," "rock," "shell." They forgot everything they had ever known. They saw layers of shifting green, a flash of pearl, a bright something beating its wings in the water and curiously kissing their ankles. Each was nothing more or less than what it was. Each was a mystery past comprehension, seeming to encompass all things.

They saw each other, and were surprised.

They drifted for a day and a night. Early in the morning of the second day, they drifted into sight of land. The land had a familiar aspect; they recognized the skyscrapers and smokestacks of their own city. They scrambled up the smooth stones of a breakwater and followed it past a mooring where white boats bobbed in the sun. Their backs to the lake, they followed the sidewalk out of the marina, up a hill, past the ballpark, past banks and county buildings, past cinemas and laundromats and luncheonettes.

When they reached the apartment, the woman held the dustpan while the man swept, until together they had cleaned up all the words.

Jessica Schabtach

✷

Carnal Knowledge

Well, I'd gotten rather good at picking up men in cafés, and it was June, and I was hungry, and my divorce wasn't yet final. I was at the café on 21st, the one with the big French doors that open right onto the street, drinking iced coffee and reading Proust, or maybe I was reading *about* Proust. Normally I chose the guys by their reading material—Virginia Woolf got me into what I thought was a one-night stand but which turned into a one-year relationship, and Henry Miller got me married—but that day there were no literary types around, just a pretty dark-eyed boy in leather pants. He was glancing desultorily through the newspaper. "Have you got the movie page there?" I asked. I already knew what time the movie I wanted to see was playing—that was why I was killing time at the café in the first place—but that was the best opening line I could think of. Not stellar, but it worked. We talked—oh, I don't know what we talked about. Movies, I guess. He'd never heard of Fellini. I invited him to come see the Mastroianni film I was going to see, but he said he had a date. So he gave me his phone number and I walked up the block to the movie theater, feeling pretty cute in the little blue sleeveless dress I'd bought the day before.

What the hell, I thought, and the next day, to our mutual surprise, I called the guy up. He was a little cagey on the phone, but we agreed to meet for lunch out on Belmont. I had to beat it out of the house to catch the bus and get there on time. I hurried too much and I was early and he was late and I had to sit at the Formica counter waiting, drinking lukewarm iced coffee from one of those red plastic cups they used to have only in pizza parlors. He did turn up, though, carrying a Gore Vidal novel with a trashy-looking cover. We sat at a booth. There was some difficulty about ordering—he had a wheat allergy, and the place specialized in pancakes—but it got straightened out.

He had a funny way of talking, as if he were conducting an interview, which made me kind of nervous. At first I didn't think he had any sense of humor, but later I thought he was just extremely deadpan; I'm not sure which one was right. In either case I felt like I was being interviewed for a job I was no longer sure I wanted, and I started squirming on the vinyl seat. Even when I started asking *him* questions I didn't feel like I was learning anything about him; he was as bland and smooth as the back of a plate. But he did have pretty brown eyes and nice hands, which count for a lot in a boy.

Being nervous, I chattered maybe a little too much, trying to fill up the gaps in the conversation as it became apparent that we didn't have much to talk about; and maybe I came off as a little flighty; and maybe he was put off as well as titillated by my having asked him out; and maybe I shouldn't have made such a big deal about us both being Geminis. Still, I was a little startled when he asked "So, is there anything I should know about your mental health?" and I just said "What do you mean?" and he said "Anything that might, say, make me think twice about letting you know where I live."

Well, I was a little startled, but we were still in big boss/humble applicant mode, so I started explaining apologetically well, yes, I do get depressed sometimes and that was a pretty bad spell I had last spring but I never got violent toward anybody else no never— Then I stopped and said "Why do you ask that anyway?"

"Well," he said, "I think I tend to attract Unbalanced People."

I started laughing. "Well, what do you think that says about *you*?" I asked.

He took this very seriously. "I tend to be very stable emotionally," he said solemnly, "and I think people are attracted to that."

Well, I wasn't so sure about that, but all I wanted was to fuck the guy anyway, so I decided to let it ride. "So tell me about these crazy women," I said.

They were pretty crazy, I guess. The chick he'd had the date with the night before claimed to have multiple personality disorder. Her second personality came to light when the first one turned into a junkie. And he'd lived for a while with a pathological liar, "but her lies didn't really affect me," he said. "She only lied about big things, like money and her past." And his college girlfriend tried to manipulate him, he felt, with her repeated suicide attempts.

By this time we'd paid the bill—he paid, which was nice, and unusual for a guy these days—and we were walking up Belmont toward his house. "So should I be worried about going to your house?" I asked. "How do I know you're not an ax murderer?"

"Oh I am," he said. "It's hell finding roommates."

But his house was nice, except for the two rats in the cage in his bedroom. I've never liked the smell of rats, even clean ones. It was an old Craftsman-style house with big comfortable rooms and dark wood floors. He showed me all over, except for the basement, which was, he said, where he kept the bodies.

"So what do you want to do?" he asked me after I'd seen the house.

"I don't know; what do you feel like?"

He shrugged. "Since I'm on vacation I'd prefer just making out all afternoon. But I can show you pictures if you'd rather."

"Must one exclude the other?" I asked. I sat down on the edge of the bed and he handed me a big photo album. Baby pictures...pretty mom in seventies peasant dress...school pictures ...college pictures...pathological liar girlfriend.... He unfastened my wristwatch and put it on the nightstand before he kissed me, but he didn't take off my glasses. The album slid off my lap. We rolled over on the plaid flannel sheets and he had at least the first layer of my clothes off before he said, "I should tell you I'm sort of a born-again virgin."

"What the hell does that mean?"

"I've only had intercourse once. I'm saving myself for marriage."

"How old did you say you were?" I asked.

"Twenty-nine."

This wasn't much of a turn-on, but it sure was a fascinating psychological study, so I made him tell me about it. Religious phase in high school, shy in college, and then he got into a habit of doing everything with girls except balling them, and then it turned into a sort of fetish (though he didn't use that word). At twenty-eight he'd capitulated and gotten laid, but it hadn't been a success, so he resumed his old habits. "Most of my girlfriends haven't minded anyway," he assured me proudly.

I knew sure as hell that *I* would mind, and I told him so. He listened politely, but he was arrogantly certain he would prove me wrong.

We didn't have time to find out that afternoon. He had to leave at five o'clock for his ballroom dancing class. It was still hot out, so he put on shorts and shiny black shoes and black socks, a combination that made him look like a pederast. His motorcycle was in the shop so we caught the bus. I went along to the dance at the Crystal Ballroom, and danced with blissfully closed eyes in the arms of pudgy brilliant old dancers and with nervous open eyes in the arms of clumsy sweaty svelte young ones. After the dance he walked me to my bus stop. We didn't kiss goodnight.

That weekend, or maybe it was the weekend after, we took a picnic up the Gorge. His motorcycle was fixed by then. He made me wear his leather pants, which had Kevlar in the knees and fell down to my ankles when I stood up, and I wore my old leather jacket and the bad-girl boots my husband had bought me on our second anniversary. Being on the motorcycle was even better than dancing with the very best dancers. I wrapped my arms around his waist and surrendered to the intoxication of wind and speed, shooting through the light-shadow-light of the forest. We ate our picnic at the old stone observatory and then kept driving on up to Shepherd's Dell. We hiked up past the lower waterfall to the pool at the foot of another, even prettier and noisier waterfall. He wanted to go skinny-dipping, but there was a family there, with kids, so we sat on the rocks in the sunshine. There was a steep cliff face on the other side of the stream and it was like sitting at the bottom of a bowl, watching the sun move slowly along the rim of stone. I'd brought a volume of Hopkins and I read aloud to him from it, shouting over the noise of the waterfall—"Binsey Poplars" and "Ribblesdale" and "That Nature Is a Heraclitean Fire and of the Comfort of the Resurrection." I don't think he got it, even though he was supposed to be a hell of a lot more religious than I was.

Finally the family left. I could see another group climbing up, but we were impatient by now so I stripped anyway and so did he. He jumped right into the pool at the foot of the falls and paddled about. I only got in about waist deep before my teeth started to chatter. My nipples were already turning blue without even touching the water. So I climbed out again. He was mad. "I thought since you didn't mind taking off your clothes there'd be no problem," he complained.

"I may be an exhibitionist, but I'm not a masochist," I snapped.

I'd hardly touched him all day, except through two layers of leather on the bike, but we started getting into it pretty hot and heavy when he dropped me back at my apartment. I had to go to a dinner party that night, though, so I threw him out so I could get ready. But he invited me to come stay the night after dinner.

I guess I figured I might as well bring things to a head, so to speak, so after my dinner downtown I got on the Number 14 bus instead of my usual Number 8. I walked up to his place from Hawthorne. It was a beautiful night, warm and scented with the blooms of flowers whose names I didn't know. He was sitting in a rocking chair on his front porch; he had a guitar on his lap but he wasn't playing, and he was smoking a cigar, and every now and then a little light breeze would ring the wind-chime. He was drinking vodka, which surprised me. "I thought you didn't drink," I said.

"I'm learning," he said.

"Don't you know vodka's made out of wheat?" I said.

"Potatoes," he said.

"Not that kind," I said. "See, their logo is a little wreath of wheat."

"Those are potato leaves," he said. I let it drop.

I smoked some of one of his cigars. I was still full of wine from dinner, but I drank some of the vodka, too, which was really nasty, and not improved by the supermarket-brand grapefruit soda with which he was mixing it. He played the guitar a little bit, and he played pretty well.

Finally we put out the cigars and poured out the vodka and went to bed. On the nightstand was a beer can which the junkie half of the split personality had left there a day or two before. The rats were awake.

We must have rolled around for hours. I knew I wasn't going to get off so I didn't feel a huge obligation to get *him* off, but I petted him politely. He was determined to prove his virility without betraying his resurrected virginity. Finally I got bored and pushed him away and pulled up the sheet. I think he was upset by his failure to get me off, but he didn't say so. He didn't say much of anything, really—just turned his back and went to sleep.

Well, I knew for sure it was all over now, and I thought about getting up and walking home. We were miles away from my house, though, and I missed sharing a bed with someone even more than I missed sex, so finally I threw a shoe at the rat cage to shut the fuckers up and I cuddled up against his big flat unresponsive back and went to sleep.

He gave me my walking papers first thing in the morning, before coffee even. He said we weren't "sexually compatible." "Well, I could have told you that!" I cried. "In fact I did tell you that, days ago." He had put on plaid flannel pajama bottoms and was lying on the plaid flannel sheets. The plaids didn't match. He said he was perplexed by my physiology. I said I was perplexed by his psychology. He had a great big plastic bowl full of cherries sitting on the bed in front of him, and as we talked he was eating cherries and spitting out the pits. "I think in the long run my virginity will be worth it," he said primly.

"You aren't a virgin," I said. He stuck out his tongue. On it rested a cherry stem tied in a perfect square knot.

I got dressed in the white embroidered crepe dress I'd been wearing the night before. It looked a little strange in the morning. Without getting up he asked if I wanted some coffee, or some breakfast, but I said no thanks, I had to get home. Then I walked up to Belmont and caught the bus downtown.

Nina Shengold

Off the Road

The house I remember the best was a beat-up chrome trailer in the woods past Rock Bay, where we lived until I turned seven. You got to our place by a long muddy spur off the regular logging road. The roadsides were choked with slash, salmonberries and Devil's Club, so thick and close it was like a green tunnel. Whenever it rained, which was always, the Studebaker got stuck in the rut where the creekwash ran over and Daddy or Jack had to hump to the shed and get chains. Puddles stayed in the ditches so long I'd find tadpoles half turned into frogs. Once Jack brought home a steelhead he swore he caught right in our road.

Jack was twenty-two back then, scrawny and tall with red zits in his beard. He was Daddy's kid brother. He used to sit down with a road map and read the names off it like it was a poem. "Ladysmith. Chilliwack. Woodpecker. Hixon. Clo-oose. Can you dig that? Clo-oose, with three O's and a dash in the middle!"

These towns were all near us, I guess, but we never went anyplace new, except when we had to change houses. One time we drove out to a place called Tofino, because Daddy thought part of who I ought to be was a girl who had swum in the ocean. "I'm taking this kid to the edge," he told Celia, "I don't want her mind to be landlocked."

Celia asked how would we pay for the gas and whose car were we going to take since the Studebaker's transmission was shot. Daddy said that was just the kind of literal-minded petty-bourgeois thinking he wanted to free me from. Celia said fine, maybe the earth goddess Gaia will pay for the gas. Fuck the damn gas, Daddy said, and she said fuck you. It probably turned into a pretty good fight but Jack scooped me up then and took me outside. It was pissing down rain so we went to the woodshed.

It was a ramshackle three-sided structure of faded gray lumber. Only two of the walls made it down to the ground. It was muddy inside. A bunch of the chickens were clumped around in there and Jack shooed them out. Daddy's axe was chunked into the stump round. Jack rocked on the handle until it came free and then set it aside. He took a bandanna out of his pocket and spread it out on the chopping block and said that was my throne. Raindrops spattered and drummed on the ridgey tin roof, rolling off in rows where the front wall would have been if there was one. The rain made a wavery screen. Looking through it, the trailer and trees seemed to shiver.

"Is he going to hit her?" I asked Jack, "Is that why we're out here?"

Jack said, "Of course not, Laurel, they're talking about car gas. You don't hit a person for that." He unfolded his map. "Look. Here's Tofino, you see, on the west coast? We're going to drive clear across Vancouver Island, one side to the other."

The door to the trailer banged open and Celia ran out in the rain. We watched. Daddy came to the door with a lit cigarette. The way that he held it, his hand covered all of his face but his eyes. They were shiny with pain, like a dog that's been punished.

A couple days later we left for Tofino in Hoot Zimmer's old pickup. It was great to be out on the road going somewhere. Daddy was driving, one hand on the bottom of the steering wheel and the opposite elbow thrust out of the wide-open window, wind riffling the sleeve of his faded plaid shirt and pulling strands loose from his ponytail. He had a bottle of beer stuck between his legs and sometimes he picked it up, swigging. Jack sat on the right in the same exact posture, but holding a road map. Celia was wedged in between them. I climbed back and forth between her lap and Jack's. Our dog at the time was a Malamute-Chow mix named Frodo. He stood in the back of the truck behind Jack with his tongue hanging into the wind.

The sun was out full and the sky was amazingly blue like the sky in a postcard. I saw a bald eagle perched on a spar tree. The wet oldgrowth woods sent up steam. The grownups all sang and Jack banged a loud rhythm on the outside of the truck door.

Let the circle be unbroken
By and by, lord, by and by
There's a better world awaiting
In the sky, lord, in the sky.

It was a song about burying your dead mother in a box but they sang it real upbeat and happy. The road roared under the truck tires, spitting up gravel. It wound around bend after bend, going higher and higher. Sometimes through a break in the trees we saw mountains with snow on the tops of them.

It was my sixth birthday. Before we took off for Tofino, Daddy made us all pancakes. He dribbled the batter onto the griddle in shapes of the letters of my name. I ate up both L's with butter and maple syrup and the A with wild gooseberry jam. Celia wrapped up the R, U, and E in a blue-jean scrap napkin for later. I was chewing on the R when the pickup truck got to the top of a hill. Daddy slammed on the brakes. "There she is, goddammit! There she goddamn is!"

Way far away was a flat line of shiny gray-blue. It was the Pacific Ocean. Daddy leaned hard on the horn and Jack let off a wolf howl and Frodo in back started barking like crazy. We all piled out of the truck. Celia said, "Shouldn't we pull it onto the shoulder?" but no one paid any attention. A log truck drove towards us and passed with a roar and a huge blast of wind. Frodo ran after it barking and Jack danced in the road. Daddy stood proud with his ropy tan arms around Celia, his lips buried deep in her shiny black hair. Then he reached down and swung me up. First I was kneeling and clutching his head, and then I stood all the way tall, my bare toes on his flannelly shoulders.

"Hi ocean!" I yelled, and I put my right hand in a fist way up over my head the way I'd seen Daddy and Jack do. And I fell.

They say I blacked out. I remember some parts of us driving: the dark wetness that seeped from my forehead, the downhill rush and the hurtling curves, the roar of the wind through the pickup cab, wind through my split-open head. Jack flipped through his maps shouting highways and distances. Daddy drove us careening downhill and due west towards the ocean.

Ucluelet was a crab-fishing town, not too big, mostly Indians. Jack leaned out of the truck window bellowing, "Doctor! Doctor! Where's there a doctor??" Some kids drinking soda pops pointed and somehow we got to one. It was a flat reddish building with walls of fake brick. The inside was tan and the curtains had pictures of ducks. The girl sitting at the front desk asked to see an insurance card. Daddy said we'd pay cash and gave her an address we'd lived at two years ago. He shot me a don't-say-a-word look and told the receptionist my name was Carol.

My head had a long gash but not very deep. It took seventeen stitches. The doctor, a wrinkled old Indian with wheezing breath and aluminum teeth, sewed up my head using heavy black coat thread. It hurt and I kicked him. Celia was clutching my hand. When it was all over the doctor said I was a brave girl and gave me a lollypop wrapped up in plastic. I'd never seen one before. It was shiny and green.

"What do I do with this?"

"Suck it," the doctor said.

"Suck you too!"

The doctor frowned, turning to Jack. "Your daughter, she got a rude mouth."

"She's *my* daughter," Daddy corrected him. "She can say what she wants."

The doctor glanced at him, then turned towards Celia. "A head cut, you want to be careful in case of concussion. How long was she out for?"

The three of them looked at each other. No one wore watches.

"Maybe two or three minutes right after the fall," said Celia. Her voice sounded strained. "And then in and out." She grabbed hold of me, clutching my hand again.

"I'm okay," I said, "Don't go insane." Celia didn't let go.

"Better not move her," the doctor said, "Not on these bumpy roads. Better to wait, keep an eye out. Let Carol rest up and I'll check her tomorrow."

We couldn't afford a motel. There wasn't one anyway. The doctor went out to a bar and made phone calls. Finally he came back and said we could sleep in the church. He gave us directions, along with his home phone to call up if anything happened, like headaches or seeing things double. He lived at a logging camp twelve miles away.

"Bring her by in the morning," he said, "And I'll give you thumbs up."

Daddy carried me out to Hoot's truck. Celia got in the driver's seat and handed the page of directions to Jack.

"What?" Daddy said, "You're not planning to *go* there?"

"Of course I am."

"Sleep in the *church*? Are you nuts?"

"But the doctor said—"

"I don't care what that dried-up old witchdoctor said. Let's get Laurel home."

"He said she needs rest."

"She can get rest. It's noon, for Christ's sake. We'd be home before three."

"No." Celia shot out the word like a bullet.

Daddy looked down at me. "What do *you* want?" His blue eyes demanded an answer. My forehead was throbbing. I had to choose who to make mad at me.

"My name isn't Carol", I told them. "I want to go home."

That might have been when Celia started to hate him. My head healed okay and my bangs hid the scar. A medical doctor in Campbell River took out all the stitches and said I was lucky, whoever had done those had sure known his business. A month or so later we drove to Tofino, just Daddy and me.

I did plenty of things with just Celia, or Jack, but I never spent time with just Daddy. It made me feel grownup and special. He didn't goof or tell Indian myth stuff like Jack would have done, and it wasn't just everyday chore and food talk like Celia. Daddy was solemn, respectful, a little embarrassed. He scanned my face anxiously, looking to see was he doing all right. I was used to him loud and self-confident, booming through the trailer in suspenders and boots, grabbing Celia and kissing her, making pronouncements. I never in five million years would have thought of him shy.

We were there. Daddy got out and stood with his back to me, pissing onto a driftlog. He helped me step down from the truck. "Do you need to go?"

I nodded and crouched, spraying into the sand on the edge of the parking lot.

Daddy took hold of my hand and we walked towards the ocean. It sounded like thunder. The sand seemed to swallow my shoes. Every step I felt like I was sinking down farther.

"It's hard to walk on," I said. Daddy reached for me as if he was going to swing me up onto his shoulders, but didn't. He looked at my forehead. I guess he thought I would be scared, or else he was. He said, "We'll go slow."

The beach was a long half-moon curve striped with dead whips of kelp. A couple of seastacks loomed out of the surf. They looked huge in the mist. Daddy said I could take off my clothes if I wanted. We both did. The wind stung our skins as we walked towards the water.

Daddy said, "Taste it," and I dipped my hand. It was so salty I spat. He knelt down and cupped his two hands in the seafoam. He touched his tongue to it and then flung the handful straight up so it rained over both of us. "Ocean!" he yelled, "Mother Ocean! The cocksucking motherfucking damn *sea*!"

It was too cold to swim, but we splashed and kicked water and shouted until we got hoarse. We dug razor clams and drew murals with sticks.

The tide was on its way out. We could walk all the way to a boulder that only a short time before was surrounded by waves. It was covered with rows of blue mussels and barnacles drying out with a weird hissing whine. Daddy showed me a rock pool with gray-green anenomes and puffy dark red starfish. The barnacles clustered together so tightly I could hardly see the rock.

"Brooklyn," said Daddy. He stared at the sinking sun. I almost thought he had tears in his eyes, but it must have just been from the wind. After a minute he turned and we walked up the beach. I had to run to keep up with him.

Brooklyn was someplace that Celia had come from. I can't ever remember calling my mother anything different, like Mama or Mommy. Her name was just Celia, like Daddy's was Daddy, though Celia and Jack called him Neal. Brooklyn had smells that I couldn't imagine, said Celia, and all kinds of noises. She was brushing my hair out. Cars lined up in rows and the houses in rows and on top of each other like cordwood. Car horns honking and radios going and all different languages people were shouting, Italian and Spanish. Fat sweaty women with big bare arms leaning and shouting out windows to the street which was jammed full of taxi cabs bumper to bumper, and only as far as from our trailer to the woodshed was a whole 'nother row of buildings and noises and potbellied men in their sleeves. People drank beers on the steps or on something called a fire escape that had cast iron stairs folded up on the front side of buildings that people escaped from. No matter how late it would never get all the way dark 'cause of so many lights that were lined up in rows down the rows full of streets. It sounded like heaven.

The tone in her voice was like she was trying to make herself grateful to leave. Celia said it was always so noisy, even the middle of the night there was traffic and people up late playing radios and TV sets and buying new food at the store. She was quiet awhile. Then she bent down and kissed my scar and sang me a song that started I See My Life Come Shining and ended up over and over with I Shall Be Released.

When the weather got hot, Jack went to a pawnshop in Rock Bay and traded his axe for a telescope. He'd decided he wanted to learn all the stars. Jack liked knowing things' names. He had bird books and plant books and wildflower books and was constantly hauling them out of his backpack to look up some new kind of duck. Those clear summer nights we sat out on a scratchy plaid blanket with unfolded star maps and traced constellations.

"Leo," said Jack. He looked through his eyepiece, then back at his chart. "Brightest star Regulus. *Regulus*. Sounds like a Roman general with hemorrhoids. What a ridiculous name for a star. Let's call it Ingrid."

"Why Ingrid?"

"Why not?" Jack stood up and shouted. "Yo! Star! We're calling you Ingrid!"

Across the clearing the trailer door swung open and Daddy leaned out. The screened windows glowed softly and made squares of light on the grass. I could hear the faint sound of a crackly sax on the radio.

"Who the hell's Ingrid?" yelled Daddy, grinning.

"Get your lazy self out here!" Jack hollered back, "We're renaming the sky!"

Daddy turned in the doorway. "Hey Ceil!" he shouted inside. She came out saying, "What?" and he started to kiss her all over her neck. She giggled and slid her hand into his jeans. Then they came out and sat with us. Daddy had brought out his pouch and they all shared a joint. Jack made lists. He got very involved with it.

"Some of these names aren't really half bad. Antares. That sounds like a star. Antares. We'll keep it."

"What about Mars?"

"*Mars*! Damn! What a terrible name! Mars goes into the dustbin of history, pronto. What do you think we should call it?"

"Harry," said Celia dreamily, stoned. She had her head in Daddy's lap. She was peeling a grass blade.

Daddy's hand cupped her left breast. He said, "Harry? The red planet *Harry*??"

They all cracked up laughing. I got up and wandered away towards the woodshed. A star fell and painted a thin streak of light down one side of the sky. I made a wish on it like Jack had taught me. I wished the same wish I always wished, that I still wish. I wished we were different.

Not long after that Daddy turned thirty years old. Jack and Celia made fun and said no one would trust him now. We had our own set of holidays, living out there. There was May Day, the Solstices, Beltain, and one called the Free Anniversary that took place on August the Fourth. This wasn't the anniversary of Daddy and Celia getting married—they didn't celebrate that—but of something that Daddy and Jack had done back when we all moved to Canada.

Every August the Fourth we had a big banquet, fresh-caught salmon or something that Daddy had hunted cooked over a bonfire, and when they could get it the grownups took mushrooms or acid. Daddy made fireworks called Cocktails from Coke bottles filled up with gas and a wick. I wasn't allowed to throw Cocktails, but Jack bought me sparklers, Roman Candles, and Burning Schoolhouses from the live bait and ammo store in Rock Bay. On other holidays, like Summer Solstice, we might invite guys Jack and Daddy had worked with, or people we'd gotten used cars or new dogs from, but the Free Anniversary was always just us.

Jack and Daddy had had other names and they changed them. They burned all the things that their old names were on and picked new ones out of a book they'd both read. It had something to do with Jack's birthday and some kind of number. There was a war going on then, and Jack would've had to go kill people and maybe get killed if they hadn't changed their names. That's all I knew, and they made it feel very important and secret and grave that I even knew that. It was Life Or Death. I could never tell anyone. The part of their lives before that was over and done with, and they had a pact not to talk about it ever, not even to each other. But sometimes they would on the Free Anniversary, after the fireworks, when it got late.

"There are things you can't ever go back from," said Daddy, "Decisions that change things forever." He was cleaning his nails with the Buck knife he usually wore in a sheath on his belt. He snapped the blade shut on "forever."

"I think of them, though," Jack said, staring into the coals. "I just wonder."

Who, I begged silently, knowing the subject would change if I asked any questions. I stared at the pulsing red embers as if I was casting a spell. Daddy leaned forward and poked them till sparks and hot cinders flew up. On the far side of the circle a flame tried to start. It jumped up, burned bright for a moment and died.

Celia said, "Well, we all have each other." She sat with her arms crossed around me in her lap, resting her chin on top of my head. "We'll always have that."

Jack had an old black and white photo he kept in a carved wooden box with his stash and *I Ching* coins. A woman with pale eyes held towheaded Jack on her lap, with a teenaged and clean-shaven version of Daddy glaring beside them. The camera had cut off the man on the edge. You could just see his hand, gripping a white-painted porch rail. I used to take out that picture and stare at it, searching for clues. It was all Jack had kept. Celia had some old letters and a New York subway token that she kept in her underwear drawer with her passport and a round rubber thing in a flat plastic box. Daddy kept nothing. When he was out working, I rifled his stuff like a thief, but I never found one thing that showed he had ever been anyone else.

Daddy and Jack made their living as loggers. Sometimes they were something called choker dogs for a former bush pilot named Clater. Other times they worked with Hoot Zimmer and Free Will Jackson, doing cedar salvage in clearcuts. They used chainsaws to carve the huge stumps into rounds, and a mallet and froe to split off the rounds into roof shakes. They made lots of jokes about working as shake-rats and dogs. "Backwoods mammals," said Jack, "Lumber madmen."

Celia stayed home with me most of the time, trying to fix things like gutters and scraping the moss off the trailer and cooking our food. She tried keeping a garden. Plants grew like magic in the constant rain and got eaten like magic by magical deer. We picked pails full of berries and boiled them to jam. We stripped alder bark to smoke salmon and sassafras bark to make tea. We tended the woodpile, split kindling and kept the stove stoked. We burned paper and bones and composted fruit rinds. We changed the cars' oil. We filled lanterns with kerosene. We were supposed to do laundry by hand to save money, but most of the time we drove into town to use coin-op machines and eat things like Fritos and Cokes while our clothes spun in circles. If we were the only ones there, I could ask Celia questions. "Did Daddy and Jack come from Brooklyn too?"

"Hardly," said Celia, and clammed up, her mouth a straight line.

When the leaves started turning, Celia said I should get school and if I didn't start meeting kids my own age I was going to turn into a precocious little creep, not that I wasn't already, but worse. Besides that the trailer was too cold and wet, and somebody else could for once in their life feed the chickens and milk the damn goat which was not her idea of fun, she was sick of the whole goddamn thing.

"I didn't get married to live like a pig," she said, "I could've been dirt poor in Brooklyn." She whirled to face Daddy. "And I could've married a man who at least showed some interest in me instead of just cleaning his chainsaw all day and *don't* interrupt me, I'm nowhere near through," and she wasn't.

We moved to Rock Bay in October, just Celia and me in a dim furnished room on top of the restaurant she'd gotten a job at, Big Al's Bar and Grille. She wore the same light pink uniform as the other two waitresses, Tessie and Pearl, but it never looked right. She wouldn't wear bras and her legs were all hairy. Tessie and Pearl both wore make-up and "foundation garments" that bulged through their dresses. They didn't like Celia. They thought she was "white trash" and "loose" and what kind of a wife left her man in the woods to just fend for himself? Pearl heard that she slept with his brother, too, all in the same bed. They smoked marijuana. And as for the child....

Whenever they knew I was listening to them, they both treated me like a baby. I told them to fuck off. They did.

Celia registered me at Rock Bay Primary School with my last name spelled one letter different, and gave our address as Big Al's. She wrote Place of Birth: Brooklyn, Ontario. When the principal asked for a copy of my birth certificate, Celia looked at her hands. "I'll have to get that from her father. We're separated right now, and a lot of my papers are still out at his place. You know how that goes." The principal said I could start, and led me to an olive-green classroom with rows of wood desks and a faded red Canada flag in one corner. All the kids stared at me as we walked through the door. I sat down at the last desk and wished I was out in the woods throwing sticks for my dog.

Celia must have been screwing Big Al while I was at school. No other way could she have kept her job. She was the worst waitress in Canada. She was internationally bad. She forgot orders, she dropped plates, she spilled soup, she yelled at her customers. And she never apologized. She couldn't care less what they thought. She smoked all the time and she'd stub out her cigarettes into clean coffee cups.

Finally Tessie and Pearl went to Big Al and said they'd both quit if he didn't get rid of that hippie bitch. Big Al did. I got yanked from first grade, where none of the kids liked me anyway, and we moved back to the trailer.

That was a terrible winter. Daddy and Celia fought, as Jack put it, "like snakes in a can." Sometimes it seemed that the harder they fought in the daytime, the louder they made love at night. It sounded as if they were trying to strangle each other.

A couple of weeks after New Year's their friend Free Will Jackson went missing. He went down to the States and he didn't come back. The grownups all talked about it like I wasn't there and the talk was confusing. They used some initials that I didn't know and talked about us going under the ground, and Jack said he thought that Free Will had been in on some weather man bombings.

"Jesus," said Daddy.

"I *think* so. He kept pretty close to the vest, but I know he was running around with them back in Chicago."

"Oh man." Daddy kicked the wall. "They're gonna fry his ass. I didn't know he was Movement. I thought he just dodged."

"That too," said Jack. "He was a pretty serious outlaw."

"What the hell was he thinking of, going back down there?"

"His family."

"His *parents*?"

Jack shook his head. "Wife and two babies. She wouldn't come with him. He missed them like crazy."

"Damn," Daddy said and sat down. Celia was watching him closely. "How did you know all this? Will never said squat to me. When did you get to know him so well?"

"I didn't. One night at the Dewdrop, a couple weeks back, Free Will beat me at pool. We got shitfaced, we talked. That's all I knew him. I don't even know how he picked up that name."

"Fuck it. Not anymore, man. Free Will."

They got drunk. Usually when Jack and Daddy got drunk they got rowdy, but this time they just sat with the bottle between them. Every so often one or the other would reach out and pour. After a couple rounds Celia got up and went into the bedroom. She told me, "Get ready for bed," but I didn't. I wanted to see what would happen.

Daddy rolled up a Drum cigarette in his fingers and smoked it right down to the nub. It was dark in the trailer, no light but one candle stuck in a beer bottle in between him and Jack. In the flickering light both their faces looked old.

Suddenly Daddy got up and walked straight for the door. The way he walked drunk always scared me. The parts of his body seemed hardly to move. He plowed through the air as if it was a brick wall and he was a bulldozer, and if you got into his way you'd be dead. He took his .22 down from the gun rack and went outside, slamming the door. We just sat there. The silence went on for a year. Then there was a single, echoing shot and a sudden clatter of chickens and barking dogs. The door of the bedroom banged open and Celia burst in, wild-eyed, clutching her bathrobe around her. She snapped on the lantern switch.

"What did he shoot?" she screamed, "WHAT DID HE SHOOT?" Jack got up and grabbed her to calm her down. Daddy came in. He was holding the gun by the barrel, loose in one hand, almost dragging it, like a batter who's struck out.

"Sky," he said. His eyes darted towards Celia's. "I had to shoot something."

The next morning I went to get eggs, and one of the hens scrambled off her high roost in a panic and got her feet tangled up in my hair. Her wings beat my head and I screamed so loud Celia came running. The hen was long gone by the time she arrived.

"I'm fine," I said, rubbing the blood from my hair, "It was just a dumb chicken."

Celia knelt on the muddy straw, holding my face in between her hands.

"Laurel, you should be in school. You should meet other kids. You should see things." She looked at me right in the eye and demanded, "Do you like your life?"

I was too scared, too surprised, to say anything. "Yeah," I said. "Sure."

Celia let go of me. "You don't know shit," she said.

That was as close as she came to discussing it with me. I don't think she even discussed it with Daddy. It was as if she had simmered so long that she'd simply boiled dry. One evening at supper she doled out the yams, plunked the casserole dish on the table and said she was leaving. She was taking me out of this dump.

I still don't know what the last straw was. I go through it over and over, trying to figure out what could have happened that never had happened before, that was worse.

There was one time when Daddy and Hoot took me fishing on Hoot's boat the Vandella and didn't pay any attention until I fell overboard, which I did sort of on purpose. Could that have been it?

Or the time the VW's home-rebuilt engine exploded in flames on the way to the laundromat. Celia got burned pretty bad and she blamed it on Daddy, for trying to fix things himself that he still needed help for.

Any number of things could have done it. Right near the end there was one fight that was different. I don't know what started it, I was asleep. The angry voices had wakened me and I put my pillow on top of my head, trying to hear just the rain drumming down and the low late-night hum of the icebox, wondering should I put clothes on and go out to the tipi where Jack slept. I was starting to drift back to sleep when Celia said something that made me sit up bolt awake.

She said, "I swear to God I'll drive into town and call up New Canaan. I'll tell your parents the whole goddamn thing."

Daddy's *parents*?? He didn't have parents.

There was a silence and Daddy said, low and intense, "If you dare..."

"What?" Celia said, "What the hell could you do to me? What would be worse than this?" Her breath caught and I heard her start crying. "This isn't what I wanted, Tom," she said, sobbing, "I don't even recognize you."

She had used his old name, the name that was over forever. Forever got flexible after that night.

Celia didn't call Daddy's parents. She called hers instead. They accepted the charges. She told them her marriage had failed and she asked for her sister Rosa's phone number in San Francisco. Once Celia decided, she never looked back. That same day she took her savings from the waitress job out of the bank and she pawned her gold wedding ring. She started to pack things. She cried when she realized how little we had that was even worth taking. I took an alderwood bear Daddy had carved for me when I was little. I wanted my clam shovel. Celia said no.

"But it's mine. Daddy bought it for me."

"Laurel, there isn't a clam within *miles* of San Francisco! It's a *city*, for God's sake! The shovel stays here and that's that."

I sat still for a minute. I watched her fold clothes. "I want to bring Nootka." This was the runt of Frodo and Wakonda's last litter. She had three black paws, a white flag of a tail and a funny splotched face.

"Honey, we can't. We'll be staying in Rosa's apartment. She doesn't have room."

"I want Nootka."

"She wouldn't like the train, Laurel. She's used to running around outdoors. She's happier here with her— " Celia stopped, biting her lip. I knew what she almost had said. With her parents. That's when I got mad.

"So am I!" I screamed, "I'm happier too! I'm not going with you. Fuck you. I can stay here with Daddy."

"Laurel— " She reached for my arm, but I dodged her.

I ran to the woods. I was looking for Daddy.

"Why don't you stop us from leaving?" I yelled at his back. Daddy turned in the path and stood staring, his hands hanging helplessly next to his sides. He looked like he'd shrunk. Finally he held out his arms. I ran into his hug and started to hit him. I pounded his chest with both fists.

"Say something! Why don't you say something!!" But he didn't. He just stood there letting me hit him.

When I had stopped hitting and crying, he held me. We stood there a long time like that on the woodpath, my face buried deep in the smell of his shirt. Then he said, "She doesn't want me." It sounded like somebody else's voice.

I looked up at him. "I do."

Daddy didn't say anything then. His jaw muscle tensed and snapped over and over, but he didn't start crying. He carried me back to the trailer. We got there as Celia was folding the last of my shirts.

Jack drove us to Campbell River, where we could get on a bus to Victoria and take the ferry to the States. The three of us sat in a line in the pickup cab watching the rain smear the windshield. Jack kept looking across me at Celia. I could see he was trying to get something said. Finally he asked, "Have you got enough money?"

"Enough to get by."

"I could loan you some."

Celia looked at him. "It wouldn't be a loan, Jack. I'm not coming back."

"I could give you some."

"No," she said. "Thanks."

"It would help."

"I know that. That's why I don't want it."

Jack glanced sideways at her, over my head. I could see his mouth harden. He nodded and turned his eyes back to the road.

"I don't want to owe anybody," said Celia, "I don't want loose ends."

"A clean break," said Jack.

"That's right," said Celia. "I learned that from him." She lit a cigarette. Her hand shook so badly she dropped the lit match. The wipers crashed over and over. Jack put on his lights, for the fog. Celia stroked my hair absently, not like she wanted to. I pushed her hand away.

Jack's pickup approached Campbell River. That was the biggest city I'd been to, back then. We went twice a year to buy groceries in bulk and big things like tools. Even with all the windows rolled up I could smell the wet stink of the pulp mills.

Jack rolled the pickup truck into the bus station parking lot. He turned off the lights and the engine. We sat facing the station's brick wall. Then Jack wrenched the door open and started unwrapping the tarp from our luggage.

Celia gave me a nudge and we got out. She held the door open for me. I don't know why that bugged me so much, but it did. The three of us walked towards the terminal, dragging our different-sized bags. There was only one suitcase.

"Here's Rosa's address," Celia said. "I gave it to Neal, but he'll probably burn it or something. I'll write to you care of Hoot. That way if you move again..."

"Yeah, we probably will, now," said Jack. He was holding her hand.

"I'll send up the papers as soon as I can. Make sure that he signs them. Make *sure*. Will you promise me that?"

Jack nodded. He looked down at the toes of his cork boots.

"I have to be free of him," Celia said, and her voice shook. She clung onto Jack. They stood hugging each other.

"Danny," she said in a broken-voiced sob. He pulled away.

"No," he said, "Jack. It'll always be Jack."

Jack picked me up and hugged me so hard I thought my ribs would crack. "Don't let anything change you," he said, and he kissed the scar on my forehead. Then he looked back at Celia and turned and was gone. He was out of our life. We stood on the bus station floor in the midst of our shopping bags.

"Come on," Celia said. She took my hand and we stood on the line for our tickets.

Victoria is real pretty with organized flowers and parks all over the place. There's a famous hotel called the Empress, which we couldn't afford to stay at, but Celia wanted for me to have seen. "After five years in that hole of a trailer it's about time you got some sense of how people live," she said. "How people *could* live."

She was dressed up, dressed for traveling. She had on a dress. I had on a dress too, a blue one she'd sewed me. It made me feel starchy and not like myself.

Celia led me up a whole bunch of stairs and into the lobby. It was carpeted with fancy patterns and crystally lights hanging way up above and a whole lot of plushy stuffed chairs. I told Celia I had to go to the shitter and she said, "Don't say that to Rosa, all right? It's the ladies' room now."

"If you say so," I said, and I went in and looked at myself in the big double mirrors. I went into a stall and took off my panties and hid them in my backpack. I turned on all the faucets at once and went back to the lobby.

Celia was inside a glass booth in a long row of phones. She was calling the ferry to find out how soon it would leave. She probably glanced out at me circling the lobby and sitting in each of the plushy maroon velvet chairs, but she didn't guess why. She finished her phone call and waved to me.

"Laurel? You ready?"

We walked down the steps, on our way to the ferry. I didn't tell Celia I'd left a damp circle of piss in the center of each maroon cushion. She wouldn't have liked that. I'd save it for Daddy.

Wendy Klein

The Bus

I've stepped from this curb onto the paved street at least a hundred times in this very spot over the past year. The traffic light, five hundred feet further on, is located at a curve in the road. I don't like to cross there. I don't like the people in their stopped cars watching me. Their headlights, competing mercilessly with the pale light of dawn, reveal too much. My left shoe has a small hole worn out on the ball of my foot. I can feel the wet packed gravel of the street. It wears an equally small hole in my stocking.

Across the street, at the bus stop, three of us huddle, each to ourselves with stiff shoulders and heads pinched low in our coat collars. We take turns craning our necks in a silent, watchful vigil and pray the same prayer as we watch longingly for the Number 15 to swing its large graceful body around the corner and open its doors. When it does, we gather and file in quickly. I offer a barely audible "thank you" to the driver as he takes my money.

I had my own car once. When I was seventeen. A used, mustard-colored Plymouth Duster, which I drove as far as my teenage imagination would take me. Like here, to where I am now, I suppose. One time, while driving away from my mother's house, my Duster picked up speed on its own. I pressed quickly on the gas as a reflex to correct the problem, then on the brake, then let up and felt the car build up speed again on it's own. I turned off the ignition in the middle of the road that day, as the car was moving. Then, in a fit of hysteria I yelled at Phil, our unsuspecting neighbor. Apparently, he was supposed to make sure my car was safe to drive. I yelled because I felt helpless and angry about gaining an independence I craved but wasn't ready for.

Weeks later, I drove my Duster through a red light that to this day I swear was green. I drove it headlong into the side of a car crossing my path. In spite of my supposed colorblindness no one got hurt. Good thing I was within walking distance to home when it happened. There was no more car after that.

Timing is everything in the world of public transportation. You learn that right away. Whether it's a bus, a plane, or an elevator, you look at your watch the minute the waiting begins and every minute after that until you're on board and the wheels are turning. It's only then that the world stops going on without you.

When I was fifteen, I had a parakeet named Misha that lived in a bright orange birdcage in my bedroom. I cut her name out of white paper and plastered it with tape, like a marquee, above the cage door. When I was home, I'd let her fly to the window and sit on the curtain rod. My mother's cat Smokey would sit on the other side of my door waiting patiently for the chance to slip inside and *whoosh*, take Misha down. The bird died one day for no good reason. I shed a few tears over how pointless it seemed, and buried her in the back yard on our side of the fence.

Now, I serve breakfast from midnight to six a.m. at the Iron Skillet, a 24-hour coffee shop on Pulaski Highway. My uniform is white, all white down to my underwear. The place is dirty. Not on the surface but underneath where the customers will never see. I use the narrow bathroom at least five times during the night to stare at myself in the mirror. I also put water on my face to keep awake. There is one other person waiting tables, a middle-aged woman named Dorothy who seems to know exactly what to do and when to do it. I feel self-consciously young and inexperienced as we sit together in a side booth not saying much, waiting for those few partied-out people to trickle in and eat something. I earn $2.75 per hour plus tips. So does she.

I left my mother's house the summer after high school ended. She drove me to the Greyhound station with two big, over-stuffed cardboard boxes barely held together with a few pieces of packing tape. They contained my entire wardrobe. Where was the luggage she liked to joke about getting me when I graduated? "You can change your mind right now," she flung into the silence as we drove. "You don't have to do this," she said. I don't remember what I said but am pretty sure it wasn't much. I was leaving her for a boy who cared nothing about me. I didn't know that at the time.

The early birds shuffle in for breakfast at around five a.m. The postman, his uniform the color of pavement at dusk, eats the same thing every morning. Two eggs over easy, scrapple cooked crispy, toast and black coffee. By now, I know he wants ketchup. He once told me I had a "dry" sense of humor. I don't know what he meant by it but took it that he thought I was dull. I usually stay a few extra minutes past my shift with the hope of collecting extra tip money. It helps take the edge off my night and off the blackness of the night outside. As I wait at the bus stop I watch the few cars go by and think about what it would be like to have that kind of freedom.

Once, the postman offered to drive me home. He said he had something to tell me. It was the morning of my birthday and he'd already given me a five-dollar tip. I really wanted the ride. It had been six months since I'd ridden in a car. I thanked him, acting as if the offer was no big deal, and turned him down by saying my boyfriend would be waiting at the stop on the other end.

On the bus, I sit close to the bus driver. It's the same man three days of the week. As we approach my stop I don't bother to pull the cord. In spite of never having looked at me directly, he knows where I get off. For a moment, the only moment of the day, I feel seen.

I walk alone to my apartment. The streetlights are minutes away from shutting off for the day. My boyfriend is asleep inside. I crawl into bed trying not to wake him. Curled in a ball, I will sleep until mid-afternoon and later scrape together enough change to buy bologna and soft bread at the supermarket down the hill.

While there I'll do my usual search through the Help Wanted section of the local paper looking for a daytime job.

Tomorrow, which is today, will come quickly. Tonight, I'll take the bus back to work. I'll walk swiftly to my stop at the corner of Cross and Goodnow and remember, without any effort, to look over my shoulder at least once every block. As I wait, I'll search out the shadowy faces of the drivers passing in their cars and imagine myself safely at my destination. The distant sound of my mother's voice will enter my head. "Take good care of yourself," I'll hear her say. When the bus arrives I will step from the yellow curb onto its bottom step with relief. I will give the driver my fare and sit two rows behind him, unbuttoning the top buttons of my coat and loosening my scarf. Then, holding my breath, I'll listen for the clunk and then the long hiss as the driver releases the brake and we glide in one long, slow, graceful movement into the dark of another day.

David Malcolm Rose

White Pine

I've heard it said that Asian bamboo can grow two feet in a twenty-four hour period, trapping sleeping birds and small animals in a living cage. Once, while checking out of the supermarket, I read that Mississippi kudzu can increase its length by the rate of a foot per hour, strangling piglets and threatening the new born. I don't know if any of this is true, but I know a Catskill Mountain white pine can grow a foot a year and keep that pace up for seventy or eighty years. And, what's more, this foot per year of growth is not hollow fish rod or flimsy vine, but solid wood, bark and pitch, with heavy branches weighted down by thousands of needles.

For seventy-five years, the pine tree behind my father's old chicken coop had everything a white pine could wish for. The soil was glacial till, assorted gravel, well drained and yet with enough tooth to hold tree roots. Such soils are not rich in nutrients but, while the trickle-down theory was a failure as an economic model it is just the kind of relationship a tree wants to have with a hen house. The fact that the chicken coop had been without tenants for the past twenty years didn't seem to be an issue with this conifer.

As I sat at my breakfast table, looking out at the fall colors, I could see the pine's twin tops sticking head and shoulders above the curtain of birches, sumacs, cedars, and lesser pines that had filled in the pasture between my father's house and my own. I could also see Dad walking with a slight limp as he emerged from the path on the far side of the garage. He wore a flannel shirt and an insulated vest against the brisk morning air, and draped over his shoulder was a short section of logging chain.

By the time my father entered the kitchen I was pouring him his traditional half-cup of coffee. He dropped the chain heavily on my chair and sat himself down in the only other chair at the small table. "Arthritis," he said, rubbing his knee.

I was being set up and I knew it. If I said nothing, my father and the chain would sit there all day. It was up to me to spring the trap. I thought of Gary Gilmore, the convicted Utah killer who chose death by firing squad over sitting in prison for years, waiting for the lengthy appeals process to play itself out. *Let's do it*, I said to myself.

"Going fishing?" I asked, extending both the coffee toward my father and my neck toward the blade. Like Gary Gilmore, I was eager to get it over with.

"Fishing for suckers and I think I just hooked a big one," Dad replied as he took his coffee without thanks. I could tell he was a bit disappointed that the game had ended so quickly. "Time has run out for that double pine below the hen house."

I looked down the hill toward the big tree. "That pine has been there a good many years," I said in the tree's defense.

"The ice stayed on the lower end of my driveway until March last spring and that tree is to blame," he countered.

"You and that tree must be about the same age," I pointed out as I the rinsed the two coffee cups in the sink. "Don't you feel some sort of connection? After all, the two of you must have been through a lot together."

"Like maybe me and that tree pulled gooseberries side by side during the Great Depression for fifty cents a day," he said.

"I wasn't suggesting anything quite that direct, but the two of you must have something in common," I offered. "Other than crusty bark."

"Now that you mention it, that smaller pine to the east is beginning to block the big tree's morning sun. I guess there's one thing we might have in common: ungrateful offspring." He stood up.

"I'll get my jacket," I said.

"Let's try and drop it right into that clearing beyond the chicken house. It'll be close to the brush heap and easier to clean up," my father said as we unloaded the ax, rope, chain saw, gas can, bar oil, log chain and binder from the back of his ancient pickup truck. He picked up the ax and held it out at arm's length by the handle, letting it hang down like a plumb bob. "It's heavy this way so we need to put a rope on it. I don't care if it hits the hen house but I don't want it down on the barn."

Over the years my father and I had cut down a lot of trees together but this one, close to three feet through the butt and a good eighty feet tall, was as big as any we ever matched ourselves against. It was a handsome pine but I could see yet another reason why it needed to come down. About fifteen feet up it forked, with the big arm on the side toward the barn. White pines are softwood and a storm could split this one at the fork, dropping half the tree on the old barn. Even half of this pine could reduce that structure to ruin.

"What do you suggest we pull it with?" I asked as I closed the rusted tailgate of the truck and rested my foot gingerly on the rear bumper.

"My old Oliver is running just fine," Dad responded as he walked toward the barn.

I undid the Bunjee cords and lifted the aluminum extension ladder down from the rack on top of the truck. I ran the ladder out full length and, using the top of it to break away dead branches, leaned it against the tree just at the fork. As I worked, I heard the old tractor fire up inside the barn. It roared, popped, chugged twice, and died. I checked on the chain saw; it was razor sharp but low on gas and oil. As I was filling the reservoirs the tractor came alive again. It backfired, coughed, sputtered and finally settled into a solid high speed idle. Lost in the sound of the tractor, I overfilled the bar oil reservoir, running oil down the side of the chain saw and over my shoe. Back in the barn the engine throttled down and I heard the transmission being engaged.

As I looked toward the barn, the old green tractor, blowing black smoke from the tail pipe, bounced out of the door and rolled across the field. The tractor and man were one as my father guided the metal dinosaur in a wide half-circle and then backed up toward the doomed tree. The old man looked as comfortable on the old machine as Roy did on Trigger. Dad shifted the transmission into neutral and adjusted the throttle lower. The black smoke stopped and the engine settled into a powerful smooth rhythm.

"Just how old is this beast?" I asked.

"1938... damn good year for tractors," he replied.

"That was during the Depression," I observed.

"There wasn't a big demand for farm equipment then so they weren't rushing when they put them together. What's more, you got to figure them fellas on the assembly line were doing everything they could not to lose their jobs."

My father stepped gingerly down from the tractor and rubbed his knee.

Together we wrapped the short chain around the tree about five feet up and cinched it tight with the binder. Big white pines will sometimes split up the trunk after you cut into them a ways. This is called shafting and a tree that shafts can do just about anything, most of which is bad. A tree that shafts can split right in two, sending half down on your truck and the other half into your shirt pocket. Or it can spin 180 degrees on the stump, jump off and mangle the chain saw, crush the gas can like a Styrofoam cup, snap the handle off the ax and then fall backwards right where you wanted it to go in the first place. Hopefully, the chain and binder would keep that from happening.

I took the rope, coiled about twenty feet of it over my shoulder, and climbed the ladder. Near the top, I stepped off the ladder and onto a branch and then worked my way up above the fork until I could get the rope around both arms of the tree. This would keep one arm from splitting off when the tractor began to put pressure on it.

It was a slow painful process involving a lot of white knuckles, and the bar oil on my shoes didn't help. Like most middle-aged men I consider a career change from time to time. Chain monkey wasn't going to make the short list. I finally managed to secure the rope but it took a good fifteen feet to go around both arms of the fork.

When I got back down, the other end of the rope was already hooked to the tow bar on the back of the Oliver and my father was at the base of the tree with the chain saw.

"You might have to drive the tractor," he informed me. "This knee hurts like the dickens every time I push down on the clutch."

"No problem," I said, "But I'm concerned that this rope might not be long enough. I used up quite a bit going around the fork. "

"Plenty of line," he assured me. "That was a hundred-foot coil of rope and this tree can't be much more than seventy."

There were some things that just didn't sit right about that last statement. It "was" a hundred-foot coil and the tree can't be "much more" than seventy feet high, for example. But your father is your father and you don't ask him the kind of questions that may show a lack of confidence.

When I got back to the tree, after stowing the ladder back on the truck, the chain saw was running and Dad was already starting the notch on the side of the tree facing the field. When the notch was finished, I took the back of the ax and knocked the wedge-shaped chunk of wood free. I climbed onto the tractor while my father went around back of the tree and started cutting down on an angle that would eventually meet the notch. Between the notch and the rope, the tree should drop right on the mark.

I worked the old tractor into gear and let out the clutch, easing the Oliver out into the field. The slack came out of the rope and small branches snapped as the noose tightened around the twin trunks high in the tree.

The rope was straining and the top of the tree shook as my father backed away from his cut. "You all set?" he shouted.

"I still don't think this rope is long enough." I yelled in reply, and pointed with my thumb back over my shoulder toward the rope.

Through the noise of the saw and tractor, Dad returned my thumbs-up sign with a smile and bent once again to his cut. The tree would go any second; there was nothing to do now but pull and hope there was enough rope.

I set the throttle on full open, let the clutch out and, leaning back, looked over my shoulder at my father. This was a bit more activity than most seventy-year-olds engage in and I wanted to be sure he cleared the base of the falling tree. There was a snapping of limbs, a quiver and then a sound like the earth splitting open as the massive pine started down toward me.

My father stepped back, looking from the tree to the tractor. Even at that distance I could see his eyes widen and his mouth go slack. I looked up at the tree and my heart banged up against the back of my throat. It was obvious now that the rope was a good deal shorter than the tree was tall.

I put one hand on top of the steering wheel and the other on the rear fender and swung myself out of the seat, free of the tractor. My feet hit the ground in a staggering run which lasted for two or three steps before turning into a clumsy drop and roll.

The giant pine came down and splintered around the old tractor, completely covering it. The earth beneath me shook and the air that blew past my face was filled with dust, dried leaves, and pine needles.

My father was right about one thing, Depression-era tractors are as tough as the men who made them. The old Oliver chugged its way out of the canopy of pine boughs and, lacking a pilot, defined a short arc across the field and into a brush heap where it stalled out.

Dad limped up, laughing so hard there were tears in his eyes.

"You always were the athlete of the family," he said. "Can't wait to tell this story."

We walked over to the tractor and inspected the right fender, hanging by a single bolt, and the badly bent steering wheel.

"Now that you mention it," Dad said, "I guess I did take about thirty feet off that rope last summer for something or other. I can't, for the life of me, recall what for."

Fred Poole

Hester Pinkham

The first place the summer world and the winter world came together was Boston. It was late winter of my second year at The Livermore School in Ashland, New Hampshire, and by then the changes in my life were like fireworks to me. I was only a 4th Former, still fifteen, but almost overnight I had mysteriously gone from being the slowest boy in the school to the most mentally nimble. I had been named to the two-man varsity debate team, joining my friend Larry Lorber, who was a 6th Former. Now Larry was poised to take up the debating scholarship he'd just won in the 1950 New England High School Championships at Bates College in Maine.

We—and this included me—were the New England champions—me and jolly, overweight Larry, who was the son of the Ashland dentist and through his family had introduced me to worlds I had hardly imagined—hundreds and hundreds of record albums, mostly 78's—played on the best equipment—Beethoven, Tchaikovsky, Chopin—played at their home in Ashland, where everyone seemed so comfortable—played also at their screen porch cabin on Lake Winnipesaukee, so very different from the big, cold houses without music where I spent my own summers, forty miles away in New Hampshire's stark White Mountains, formal houses where at dinner there were always finger bowls and the men wore tuxedos. Suddenly now I was not only bright, I was experiencing things I did not think anyone else in the family had ever seen. Casual homes, casual dress, music all the time. Justice much the time. Jews.

Now Larry and I and the debate coach, our funny and sympathetic mentor Joe Abbey, who taught English and loved the written word too—Joe was to take Larry and me for a debate just outside Boston at what I thought of as a real prep school, not our small, virtually unknown Livermore but rather hundreds of perfectly dressed students, solid tweeds, an upper class society world, stiff and formal and privileged—Latin and Greek and British constitutional history, bagpipes at important assemblies—Milton Academy.

Not so far in spirit from the formal family summer compounds in the White Mountains, whereas The Livermore School, in lake country, although Anglican and at least tentatively tweedy, was seeming more and more like the open world of the Lorber family.

At this time I was deeply immersed in a girlish girl with straight black hair named Annie Bell. We'd met and necked two months earlier at a dance at our sister school, St. Mary's-in-the Mountains. My first really passionate experience, tongues on tongues, hands on her creamy skin. We wrote daily letters—with "S.W.A.K." on the back of hers—S.W.A.K., Sealed With A Kiss. And on both of ours the stamp always upside down as a symbol of being too in love to be careful. And these letters of hers, which ended with "I love you and adore you," were always on pastel stationary. And the stationary was always heavily scented with her gardenia perfume.

Once a week at least there would also be a letter from another girl—written on heavy off-white stationary, with an embossed private school crest, no scent, stamp right side up, nothing on the back except a suburban Boston address. Small precise hand writing—like the handwriting of a much older person, I thought—unlike the great loops and swirls and I's dotted with hearts that came from Annie.

The weekly unscented letter was from Hester Pinkham, older by a year sister of Jay Pinkham, who was actually a student, a boarder, at Milton.

Although I had decided to turn my life over to young Annie—she wore strapless dresses to two school dances and put her leg right between mine as my hand went to the bare area of her back.... Although I had gotten this far in life—all the way to Annie and debating trophies after starting out as the slowest, most unpopular boy in the school—I did not think to stop writing Hester. We'd been friends since infancy during summers in the mountains—she and Jay and their first cousins Janice and Tom Colby. Actually my twin brother Matthew, the good twin, and I were vaguely related to them. Their grandmother, old Mrs. Toliver, and their parents were on a genealogy chart hanging in the telephone room at White Pines, the biggest of our family's four big summer places. The chart saying who bred who—using the word "begot"—and our own grandmother, Mims, was on the same chart, and Mother and Dad and Matthew and me too. So I was some kind of safely distant cousin of Hester's—not so close as to make it a problem. But actually there was a huge problem.

Although during the last summer we had started smiling across old people's living rooms at each other, and teasing each other by splashing at a swimming hole, I could not conceive of even holding hands with Hester. She seemed almost pretty in a kind of distinguished way but hardly girlish. She had fine tanned legs but in stiff shorts that came to her knees—and there was something brittle about her, prominent bone structure and too little flesh, and ramrod stiff posture, already a little like the tight older women at the White Pines dinner table.

Hester and her family were clearly the sort of people our grandmother Mims, and sometimes our mother, referred to as "our kind of people." They had a summer compound like ours, with separate quarters for children and nurses, and more separate quarters for cooks and maids. When I mentioned to Hester that I saw her name on the genealogy chart in the White Pines telephone room it occurred to me that I was talking to someone who would not need to ask, "What is a telephone room?"

In my letters to Hester, I boasted about my debating triumphs. I told her about the event scheduled for Milton. Hester wrote now asking for the debate coach's address. She said that although Jay was a boarder, Milton was only a few miles away from Westwood, where the Pinkhams lived. Mrs. Pinkham would write Mr. Abbey, and he and Larry and I would be invited to stay with them when we came down from New Hampshire for our David-Goliath battle with Jay's school.

All of the students at Milton, all of them in rich-looking Milton blazers, were there when Larry and I won on a stage in a hall that seemed like something belonging to a Scottish castle.

And afterwards we went to a formal dinner in a shiny dark dining room at the Pinkhams, and then Hester led Larry and me to a square dance in the basement of Westwood's Episcopal church, where all the boys had ties and all the girls were in long sleeves.

Later Larry and I were put in a spare attic room with cots for the night. We spent most of that night talking. To my pride, but also my horror, Larry said he'd never seen anything so wonderful as this world of the Pinkhams, nor a girl with such class as Hester.

This from Larry my friend from far outside the family. Larry, dark hulking rebel, with a smooth, bouncy, rosy round co-religionist girlfriend with big bright lips who came up to see him from West Hartford, Larry my companion in adventures—we'd gotten our hands on an illicit car—he and I like escaped convicts, touring southern New Hampshire without licenses, spying on lakeside parkers, doing it after midnight, long after you were forbidden not just to leave your dorm room but even to turn on a light—

Larry up here in the attic-like room of the Pinkhams solid Westwood house, now telling me where he thought I belonged.

Afterwards it never came up again, but through this night we argued on, using our debating skills, Larry also pulling age on me and insisting that I would soon see why I must give up Annie, rise to this once in a lifetime chance to get a girl like Hester.

I refuted him methodically and loudly, arguing from the evidence of strapless dresses, French kissing, what we called petting, and Annie's leg between mine at the dances. I wasn't going to give this up.

Finally Larry sighed, got into his cot bed, turned against the wall, started to snore. In the morning, at breakfast—with delicate china and crystal juice classes and heavy silver—there was such a freeze—not a word spoken by Hester herself and not much coming from Mrs. Pinkham either—that I knew Larry and I had been overheard.

H. N. Levitt

Incident at The Summer Writers' Conference

Alloway and Roberts were the first to arrive at the staff cottage late during the night of the third day of the conference. The others were out and would be expected along soon. It was the custom for staff and fellows to congregate for a little conviviality after the fuss and fury of a long day of lectures and clinics with the faithful. Alloway walked with impressive strides over the New England turf, giving a lot of consideration to his Dunhill pipe; he examined each puff carefully as though there were ideas in the smoke he was reluctant to let go.

"Yes," he said, "so it would seem," to some carefully worded remark by Roberts, who, because of his shortness was being forced into a slow trot by Alloway's brisk pace. But he hadn't actually heard Roberts' remark; he had responded only to the inflection in his voice, a lifetime habit he had cultivated to appear responsive when necessary. Alloway indulged in long, internal dialogues which would unwittingly drown out other voices, addressed to him or not. Hence, the many "ah, yes's" and "so it would seem's" that punctuated his conversation. Courtesy was for him one of the key character traits that distinguished the accomplished, professional writer from his uncivilized counterpart—that brash, unclean, boorish exhibitionist whose manners, in Eliot's phrase, "matched his fingernails," and whose work so often crudely indulged his ego without offering much else.

Alloway strode into the cottage with Roberts a step behind, but he was not really in the cottage yet; he was still out under the clouds of stars in that vast, dark New England sky, thinking through his pipe. The sitting room with its cheerful fire closed in on him some moments after he had actually entered.

Roberts was angry with himself because he knew that Alloway hadn't heard one word he had said in the last few minutes and because he, Roberts, hadn't had the guts to tell him that he knew it.

"With Fitzgerald, you see," Alloway was saying, "there is always that perfect coupling of the place with the event so that even the descriptions are carefully chosen to get the narrative across in the right mood. He doesn't write from himself; he writes to the event. There are those two great scenes in Gatsby when Nick enters the Buchanan living room—you know, the two ladies on the couch?"

"Yes," said Roberts.

"Fitzgerald invests the first scene, at the beginning of the book, with hope and promise, and at the end, the very same scene has a foreboding of despair—and all, mind you, in the descriptions of the objects in the room."

"It occurs to me that…"

"You see," Alloway said, "the event dictates exactly what the environment will be."

"I admire the absence of mannerism in him," said Roberts.

"What?" Alloway was caught off-balance, but he recovered quickly. "But there is manner, isn't there? A boyishness, an exuberant style that turns to brooding when, as they always do with Fitzgerald, prospects diminish and the early enthusiasms pall."

"What I meant was mannerism in the sense of Hemingway's preoccupation with form, the self-conscious style," said Roberts.

"Yes, of course," Alloway said, "so it would seem."

"I have in mind three kinds of style," Roberts said, "the baroque, the mannered, and the plain. In that sense I meant..."

"Another interesting aspect of the Fitzgerald technique is the presence of continuous motion. Even reflection occurs while we move from place to place. This vague, uneasy shifting of time and place is what gives his characters that sense of rootlessness, that sense of opportunities missed, and the burden of memory."

"That motion is the natural selection of a writer who shuns mannerism and lets the events tell his story!" Roberts almost shouted.

"Ah, Peter!" Alloway said, turning abruptly away from Roberts to welcome Peter Aulicino, the conference director. Aulicino in his thick, brown-bear, cable-stitched sweater lumbered into the room, drink already in hand, and a fresh, engaging smile on his big, homely, yet handsome face.

"I don't have the proper attitude toward criticism," Aulicino said. "One should have Olympian Remove, but dammit, I get mad when someone doesn't like what I write!"

The three men settled down by the fire. They were beginning to savor the conference routine after three days of what had seemed chaos. They were beginning to enjoy themselves.

"Now I know I shouldn't say this but," Aulicino whispered behind his second tumbler of scotch, "I was disappointed in Bloom's first lecture. It was a little sophomoric. That Solomon kid made some interesting points in rebuttal, didn't he?"

"Solomon? Do you *really* think so?" said Alloway.

Aulicino glanced at Roberts for support but it was not there.

"Yes, I think so," said Aulicino, plunging in. "Bloom starting his session with a lecture on the virtue of taking notes is a little too much."

"Aren't you being hard on Bloom?" Alloway asked in fine voice.

"What do you think, John?" Aulicino asked Roberts.

There was a long, uncomfortable silence while Roberts labored. "I think he was saying more," he finally said.

"Bloom?" asked Aulicino.

"No, Solomon," Roberts said. "The fellow. He made a good point about the characterization in a good story accumulating around the event. There's the incident itself, then its past history, that says what kind of people the writer will dream up. It's like your friend Fitzgerald setting the mood and action by the description of the objects in the room," he added in an aside to Alloway.

"Oh, now, I can't let that one go by," said Alloway.

Aulicino hadn't understood a word Roberts had said. He found himself wondering again, as he had the summer before, why he had asked Roberts back on staff. The man was such a complicated bore. Aulicino's wife spoke of the "perennial sedates" on staff, and the desperate need for some "seasonal uprooters" to bring some pizzazz to the conference.

In the midst of Alloway's tiresome, irrelevant response to Roberts, Donald Everett, the star performer of Mrs. Aulicino's "perennial sedates," walked in. Whatever Everett may have been to Aulicino's wife, to half the publishing world he was the "venerable editor," and to the other half, an extinct dinosaur. He saw himself as a knight in armor fighting single-handedly against the decay and breakdown of moral and spiritual values in western society (eastern was no better!) which was leading to the death of the novel. He was flaying a dead horse for all it was worth; for him, it was worth much—it gave him a reputation and high status. In his publishing house, for which he served both as chief editor and president, his associates were less susceptible to propaganda; their hearts were filled with hope as the inevitable day of his retirement moved closer. Everett carried a pipe, a long, thin Lumberman shape, that he thought went well with his skeletal face, reminded him a little of that Van Gogh painting. He too, like Alloway, used the pipe to appear thoughtful; unlike Alloway, he never smoked his.

"Very interesting, Alloway," he said after nodding to the others and taking a commanding position by the fire (he didn't drink, and he didn't like sitting in a group). "I agree. Characterization *is* the novel. This hideous preoccupation with the tedium of observable objects, and this—this—this outsider's view of human actions as though they were, as though it were manipulated by strings and the—the mere description of it were enough, this is appalling, Alloway! The novel will always be the mind turning on itself, probing its motives, presenting human behavior with insight and intelligence in the logical construction of its own reasoning. I have never been able to, I have never heard a better definition than that."

"Yes," Aulicino said, vaguely, stifling a yawn.

"And some of these people," Everett continued, "some of these people who go around ill-kempt, ill-mannered, and ill-shaven, whom we endow with fellowships, and who assault us with their half-baked, self-indulgent drivel—they should be silenced, if necessary, to allow us to continue the work of the conference."

"You mean Solomon," Alloway said.

"Whatever his name is," said Everett.

"There's a case to be made for intellectual discomfort," Aulicino said, smiling warmly and tentatively at Everett.

"Disputation is not the purpose of this conference," Alloway said.

"Hear, hear!" said Everett.

John Roberts coughed to clear his throat. "D-D-Disputation," he suddenly stuttered, "is a way to inform also."

"That kid is disruptive," Alloway bore down, looking straight at Aulicino. "He turned Connolly's lecture on meter and rhyme into a riot, he provoked Bloom with so many insolent interruptions that the poor man forgot his material, he walked out on Don Everett here, rattling the chairs as he left, and he laughed outright in the middle of John Robert's lecture. How can you defend him?" He asked Roberts as thought he were in pain.

"He made... some points," said Roberts, vaguely, his brows deeply furrowed.

"Name me one," said Alloway.

"His argument against the foreshadowing of events," said Roberts.

"But he used that against you," Alloway said. "He was screaming at the top of his voice. He was so hysterical I couldn't understand him."

"I thought l-l-later about what he meant to say," Roberts said, "and it was an interesting point."

"But he didn't say it," said Alloway.

"But he meant to say it," said Roberts.

Alloway sat back and puffed quickly on his pipe. He stared at Roberts' face as though there were something written on it. Then he took a sip of bourbon and reclaimed his self-assurance.

"I admire you, John, for that scholarly calm, that Platonic devotion to ideas that lets you excuse a man's ugly behavior. I'm not that generous."

"Oh, by all means, a man's behavior is..."

"I find his ideas equal to his manners," said Alloway.

"Well, you know, Peter," Everett waved a long, bony finger toward Aulicino's half-closed eyes, "I think it would be entirely proper to ask that person to leave the conference."

"What person?" said Aulicino, turning away from the fire to keep awake.

"Solomon," Alloway said.

"That Solomon person," Everett said.

"I don't follow you. We should ask him to leave?" said Aulicino.

"For disrupting the conference," said Everett.

"He'll do more harm than good," Alloway piped in.

"Ah, hmmm," said Aulicino, stalling for time.

Roberts spoke up in a barely audible voice. "I think it might be a mistake."

"I'm interested in what *you* think, Peter," Alloway said to Aulicino, putting Roberts away at once.

"It's a little odd to give someone a fellowship and then revoke it three days later. On what grounds?" asked Aulicino.

"Disturbing the peace," snapped Everett.

John Roberts was the first to notice Solomon. He'd been glancing out the window and he saw him pass under the light across the road, heading toward the cottage. He recognized the younger man's peculiar gait—arms pinned to his sides, body leaning slightly forward, and the whole system springing vigorously from the toes like a wound-up tin soldier. He saw the tangled shock of prematurely-greying hair, and the baggy, well-ventilated sweater that had already become a conversation piece. He saw Solomon coming but he said nothing to the others. He felt a certain kinship with him and he hoped he would do well.

The others were not so fortunate. Solomon's sudden presence in the room shocked them so severely that they fell out of character and did their best to welcome him and make him as comfortable as possible in the good, soft chair by the fire. Alloway and Aulicino looked conspicuously guilt-ridden. Everett merely waved a tentative welcome, which, for him, was an extensive undertaking. Aulicino got up and poured another drink for himself and one for the newcomer. They settled into another uncomfortable silence.

"You know, Bob," Solomon finally said to Alloway, "that stuff you dished out about putting Henry Miller's obscenity aside in evaluating his work is a lot of garbage."

"You're misquoting me!" Alloway said, his voice pitched an octave higher. "What I said is there is nothing enlightening about Miller's obscenity; the uniqueness of his work is the way he was able to reproduce himself in it. He re-created the living man with all his stupidities, lust, ambition, and his splendor. I went on further to say…"

"Lawrence made sex fair game for the novel, but he was a romantic," Solomon interrupted. "Henry Miller showed how much fun it is, and he had the guts to be clinical. In fact, he was clinical about everything—the new twentieth-century man. He took things apart and put them together again. His obscenity is the heart of his work."

"Ah, you see, that's wrong," Alloway said. "For Miller, what really comes through is his..."

"What could be more Rabelaisian than Miller mounting his girl in the hallway and reaching into her purse at the same time, fishing around for carfare to get home?" Solomon shouted.

"Will you excuse me?" Donald Everett said as he nodded perfunctorily and strode out.

Solomon ignored him. "I'll let you off the hook, Bob," Solomon said to Alloway. "You may have a point somewhere but you're way out on a limb and if we keep going you're going to get hurt."

Alloway flushed. "You haven't said anything even remotely debatable," he shrieked. "How is the hallway episode relevant? Where is the logic in your argument?"

"Now, now, Robert," Aulicino said, placing a hand on Alloway's tense arm, but he might just as well have shot him with an elephant gun at point-black range. Alloway was devastated. That slight, ameliorating remark by the conference director at the crucial moment fell on Alloways' head like a mantle of defeat. He remembered the incident years later, never forgiving Aulicino, who, in his innocence, thought he had done some good by quieting things down.

"One virtue of Miller's work," John Roberts suddenly said to Solomon, "is the absence of mannerism—that lusty, intimate, unliterary style that influenced more writings in our generation than Proust *or* Joyce."

"That's one thing about you, John," Solomon said to Roberts, "you can't get off that three-way style kick. But it's not that simple. The baroque is easy enough to pin down, and so is your mannered style. But what the hell is a plain style, John, other than the mannerism of a plain man? All writing is a kind of mannerism. The plain writer who sticks to the facts without intruding on the material ends up by intruding on the material. You can't get rid of that subjective assumption. He is there! We get everything through him. Everything *is* him. We say, 'He's done it this way either because he's dull and uninteresting himself, or he wants us to see the story in that spare, lifeless way.' In both cases we have mannered styles. You know, I think I could argue there's no such thing as baroque; there's only mannered because..."

"Now listen, Solomon, for Christ's sake, don't you think you've said enough?" Aulicino said.

"I didn't get to you yet," Solomon said, winking at Alloway and smiling at what he thought was a touch of humor. But he was very wrong. Aulicino perhaps had drunk too much, perhaps not. At any rate, the bitter scene that followed became the big story of the conference that year, and it inflicted wounds.

"You didn't get to me yet? Is that supposed to be a joke?" Aulicino said.

"You said some things about free verse, Peter, that I..."

"I mean, what the hell are we running here---a shooting gallery?"

With that, Alloway revived. "It's easy to sit back and criticize," he said to Solomon, "but it's another matter entirely to make sense. But more than that—we're not used to rudeness here. And we don't shout; we talk."

"Ah, what the hell!" Solomon said, smiling broadly and waving his free hand at Alloway. Writers should have thick skins."

"And they should clean them once in awhile," said Aulicino.

"Yeah," Solomon said, laughing.

"When's the last time you took a bath?"

Solomon sat back in his chair for the first time. He searched the faces of the others for some clue to the humor, found none (even John Roberts looked serious, though unhappy) and then merely shrugged his shoulders.

"I mean, who gives a damn about taking baths?" Aulicino weakened. "But one sloppiness leads to another. If you washed your face and combed your hair and changed your underwear and socks once in awhile your ideas might also be cleaner."

"What the hell are you, my mother?" Solomon suddenly snapped.

"I would like to go back to the point Philip made about the baroque and the plain styles," John Roberts said. "I think that would be best."

Alloway turned to him. "The time for your academic objectivity is over," he said. "We're talking about civilized behavior, intellectual courtesy,"

"Oh, balls!" Solomon said. "You guys can't be serious."

"What about what I said about free verse? What about it?" Aulicino said, his round, fleshy chin shoved forward.

"You quoted that silly Frost line about writing free verse being like playing tennis without a net, and then you..."

"Silly?" said Aulicino. "Silly?"

"There is no free verse," said Solomon. "Language is rhythm and sound. Free verse is still the poetic sensibility expressed through the rhythms and sounds of language. It's very un-free. The poet follows the laws of his Muse. Why shouldn't her laws be just as valid as the ones you guys laid down the last four hundred years or so?"

"What guys the last four hundred years?" Aulicino said.

"All you guys in the establishment. All the 'in' writers. You guys who made the rules. Well, there's a new bunch coming up and we've got some answers too. We know all yours—we've heard them a hundred times. The difference between you guys and us is that we all look ahead and it looks pretty grim, only you want to retreat to the safe ground, and if nobody bothers you, well, that'll be just fine, but we, we want to go out and cut new ground. We've got a bellyful of the past—we chewed it, we swallowed it, we digested it—it did its work, it kept us nourished for awhile, but now we got to go out there where the action is. We want to write poems that all the sick people we live with will want to read, and they'll feel it in their bones. And we want to write stories and books that say, 'Look, *this* is the way we are, not that back there, but this, this new thing, this terrible thing, this doomed thing, and we must not turn away, we must not lie to ourselves, we must be honest!'"

A sudden, heavy silence fell on the room. Solomon took his dirty handkerchief out and wiped his sweaty face. He was breathing deeply and seemed to be holding back tears.

Aulicino stood up, turned, and walked to another spot. He had put down his drink. He was tense, nervous; he didn't know whether to stay put or move somewhere else. His hands opened and closed involuntarily. He suddenly turned to Solomon with a look of pain on his face.

"How easy it is for you to talk that way," he said. "The 'in' writers, the establishment. Who the hell is an 'in' writer? We're all outsiders. The laws of the Muse against the laws of...what kind of garbage is that? Argue to the point. Stop taking pot shots. Who in this room isn't an honest man? Who wants to lie? You are the voice of chaos, Solomon. Knowledge makes you uncomfortable; you have no patience with it. Ideas assembled into theories bother you because that means somebody else was there before you. You're a professional iconoclast, a rebel, an uprooter!" Aulicino thought of his wife and quickly brushed it aside. "You protest, you argue, you revolt. It makes no difference who says what—you're against it. And you..."

"Some people learn a few things and all they do is repeat them all their lives," Solomon shouted, a touch of hysteria in his voice.

"Stop interrupting, damn you!" Aulicino said.

Then he went on to say something about "avant-garde intolerance." But he lost interest in his own thoughts. He was ashamed of the way he had shouted Solomon down, and the more he talked the more ashamed he became.

For his part, Solomon had been squelched for the first time. He couldn't understand why Aulicino had been so harsh, and it frightened him. He sat back troubled, and he knew he'd have nothing more to say. He felt trapped in the room, pinned down by the presence of the others and the droning voice of Aulicino. He began to sweat again, and he mopped his brow with the same damp, dirty handkerchief. While Aulicino was still talking he decided he wanted to leave, that he'd have to leave, and that he'd leave the next day.

Aulicino stopped talking in the middle of a sentence. He dropped off in the midst of an analogy that somehow didn't need to be made. The expression on Solomon's face, that pained look of uncertainty, of unconditional surrender, was so disturbing to Aulicino that he became angry with Alloway in an attempt to spread the blame.

"Would you please pass the goddamn cheese?" he said, as though Alloway had refused.

But Alloway missed the point. "I'll pass the bloody cheese," he said, "after I have my say! Tearing down established work is nothing new. There's no truth in the process. It's not enough to criticize doctrine. The work is the thing that speaks. You may argue against foreshadowing events in the novel," he said to Solomon, "but until your work shows how it has avoided it in an interesting and unique way, the argument is academic."

Solomon heard him and he thought vaguely that the logic was poor, but he had no heart for the debate any longer. He nodded in a friendly way to Alloway, implying the point was well made, then he rose, excused himself to Alloway and Roberts, and asked Aulicino if he might have a word with him outside.

It was a dark, busy night, pulsing with chirping crickets, croaking bullfrogs, and the bubbling of the brook just beyond the cottage. The two men stood a little to the side of the front door and nodded to a few members of the staff and some fellows who had just entered. Aulicino placed his hand on Solomon's shoulder to atone in some palpable way for his boorishness. But Solomon was unaware of the gesture; he was struggling with his thoughts.

"Peter," he finally said, "well, the fact is, I wanted to tell you sooner. I'm leaving tomorrow and I hope that you don't hold it against me—you know, the fellowship and all that—but I want to get back to work, and I don't do well talking and discussing things, and things like that. What I mean is I don't understand them. I mean, I think there's room for everybody but there's nothing but enemies in there."

Aulicino immediately objected. By this time they had started walking away from the cottage. Aulicino told Solomon that his leaving would be very upsetting to him personally, and to the others as well, but they both knew better.

They parted with a handshake. Solomon said his farewells the next day and took off. Aulicino eventually came around to seeing the incident in the cottage and Solomon's early departure as unrelated. The departure, in time, seemed more like the direct result of the kid's paranoia. Donald Everett said he was satisfied with the way things had gone. Alloway was confused. When he thought of it, much later, he remembered certain attractive qualities in Solomon he had overlooked, the main one being his commitment, his total commitment. You couldn't put that down. Alloway still thought his arguments were specious, but perhaps he had been hasty in his judgment of the guy. John Roberts was moved and disappointed in what had happened. He had enjoyed Solomon's criticisms, though he hadn't agreed with them, but he had also liked the man.

Del Marbrook

Ice Storm, 1999

They were helping themselves to the president, the hyenas of the House pawing their kill in the trough of the posturing boars of the Senate while the buzzards pressed and cawed. The disquietingly porcine congressor from the South was making the constitutional case against priapism when a great whim moved the glazier to crystallize the overheated bestiary, sparing it momentarily from yapping itself to death. Even the hoarse buzzards were grateful.

The ice storm made everything beautiful, but the news was the inconsiderateness of the beauty. He felt the glazier's sorrow and remembered making castles in the sand.

And when the blessed silence turned to sirens' wail, all the broken limbs and severed arteries of the former incivility lay exposed as after a quake, and even as people huddled in their powerless world, the trolls, grotesques and nyes were heard disputing their meal on The Hill.

Washington is a bad town for people who hear people think. They should avoid it. It draws them to the deafening attributes of drink. Nothing overheard in that swamp of talk emboldens the soul to transcend, everything heard is suspect and dank.

As the fetor clawed at the ozone hole, he felt his life compress, himself jammed out. He was jogging past the power plant on the Virginia side of the Potomac. Chuff, clang, hiss, it said, and he decided then to close Others, his rare book shop on Capitol Hill. Chuff, clang, hiss. The sound of a place whose chief product is words. Yes, it would be better to put his carcass out to bleach away from the chuff of hypocrisy, the clang of rancor and the hiss of deceit. Nothing could wean these posturers from their addictions except—should he risk a thought so humble?—the prayers of the meek.

Here he could see as far as Hatteras light could reach and had as much purpose, but he couldn't discover it by naming it. When he did discover it he had no more questions in him. He'd come to do a thing too humble for words. Until his savings and his life ran out.

She noticed them four years ago. The wind erases them, the ocean drowns them, feet derange them, crabs mine them, but from Rodanthe to Salvo they appear as faithfully as tide: bas-reliefs in the sand. Octopuses with arms interlocked. A dolphin in headset. Camelot streaming her gonfalons. He used food dye, shells, seaweed and driftwood, and nothing endured more than twelve hours.

She'd come to Salvo to die, but a dream convinced her she had a few things to do. She dreamed she was wearing a white burnoose and a cheche, one of those North African turbans. She was standing on a morning mist stirring a cauldron with an oar. I'm an alchemist, she thought. I must find proper elements.

Old age showers you with clarities and simplicities if you don't struggle. Her study of the sandman's ephemera is one of these graces. She finds them at the tide line, in the sand coves of the grass line, in the arroyo between the barrier dunes, framed by the taffrail of a wreck, cornered by tufts of gaillardia. Her elements. Her camera her alembic, her eye its elixir.

Cordgrass binds the dunes against the wind. That's the given of the place, punctuated by ground juniper. People who look their weight in the cities and the suburbs blanch and tear loose here. In his habitual khakis he's as spectral as a sand crab. He sits so still in knurls of grass that black racer snakes feel safe to slither under his legs. He watches the sea froth, the tease of the tide, the sandpipers' daft chorus line, the phalarope's dervish whirl, families and lovers upanchored, not as a voyeur but simply because he has learned to sit still. In the ecstasy of this gift, his face and arms streaked with green, he is moved to sculpt the sand.

Now, watching her investigate his work, as he has for more than a year, as the Croatans watched the English encroach, he sees imaginings swarm her head like gnats. He sees her heartbreak in the vulnerability of his work. He hears her stalking camera whine and snick, exulting in his capture and imprisonment.

Later, when the renters come, he sees her trophies in a gallery, his work pinned like dead butterflies. He shakes his head. Lonely as she is, as he is, she is not for him. He isn't as visible as he'd been in Washington and she's a trapper of visibilities. She doesn't know who the sculptures are for. She doesn't understand for whom he works.

That night he flies far beyond light's reach. Nothing can bring him back except the sob that wakes him.

Marta Szabo

Tampered With

I am going to work. I am 21 years old. I have just driven from New York to LA with Jeffrey in an old Mercedes Benz he inherited from his Uncle Eliot. I am living in Hollywood now with Jeffrey in a small white stucco cottage surrounded by thick greenery and flowers called "birds of paradise" even though this is a city and it's still winter time.

I go to work by bus because the Benz belongs to Jeffrey. He's just not the kind of boyfriend who shares. We came here so he could be a film director. While he's waiting for that to happen he gets a weekly check from his dad so he doesn't have to do anything dumb like go to work. Sometimes he needs the car during the day to go record shopping. He likes to go to second-hand record stores. It takes a long time because he has to flip through boxes and boxes of used records that are in alphabetical order, looking for the one song he needs to finish the tape he's making. So in case he needs the car I take the bus.

This morning Jeffrey has left out a letter to mail from my office where I can zip it through the Pitney Bowes postage meter for free. I got this job out of the newspaper as soon as we got here. I am a secretary for a man named Larry who wears short-sleeved shirts with ties and tie clips. He sells yellow pages advertising. When I go to parties and people ask what I do I have to say I'm a secretary. I can see them fade away on me immediately and I don't blame them. I wish I could say I'm a writer.

My desk at work feels like a prison, my days stretching and stretching, empty empty empty, lunch breaks, a letter to type, the receptionist painting her nails and talking about what's on sale. I try writing stories on yellow legal pads so my days are more than just things I check off. I make up a story about a man who lives alone with pictures of girls plastered over the walls of his apartment. At night they whisper to him. They part their lips. They part their thighs. I've gotten this far and don't know what comes next. I like writing about crazy people. I put in the sex because Jeffrey doesn't take anything very seriously that doesn't have drugs or sex in it.

I pick up Jeffrey's letter and as I carry it to the bus stop up on Sunset Boulevard I examine it. It's addressed to Kerry. Kerry is tall and exotic and has already turned thirty. She knows where to get any drug you want. She's been to India. Overland. She's lived in Paris and drives a red Triumph convertible. She's done everything I haven't. Jeffrey would sleep with her if she wasn't so much in another league. She writes him letters too. Jeffrey has shown me how she signs them. A kiss in gold lipstick.

I press the envelope smooth as I walk so I can read through it. I see my name. I knew I would. Jeffrey is writing to Kerry about how hard it is to be with me, that I'm depressed too much, that he wants to have other relationships, how he's always wondered whether it's better to talk about affairs or keep them secret. Jeffrey is so open with his friends.

My walking becomes automatic—my stepping up onto the bus, my sitting, my looking through the window at nothing. I am no one. I am not interesting. I am not a writer. I'm not witty and traveling and getting phone calls all day. I work nine to five as a secretary and I get there by bus. I tell my boss I'm sick and turn around and go home again.

Jeffrey won't be there today. He's with Steve hanging lights for a student film and hating it.

I will be alone. I can do it. If I don't do it I will have to stay here in this silent living room with the same hot LA sun outside, the sound of traffic on Fountain Avenue, stuck.

I stand in front of the bathroom sink. I take the razor blade. I cut one wrist. A red line of blood. I close my eyes. Cut the other wrist. Fast but not too deep. I look through eyelashes. I see inside the skin to veins and blue under-skin things I know I am not supposed to see and it's enough. I stop. Tape it all up with a couple of band-aids. I didn't finish, but now I can call Jeffrey. I get to be fragile, he gets to be strong. I tell him I cut my wrists because I read through the envelope and he says he'll come home early. We'll get high. He'll make dinner. I am home again. The spell is broken.

We are not surprised. This is all a little ordinary. Not quite as ordinary as every other day, but nothing to make a voice rise. After all, Jeffrey cut his wrists years ago and even got as far as getting in the tub, so he is still way ahead of me.

"You know," says Jeffrey before we hang up, "you shouldn't read other people's mail," and what can I say? He's right.

Marilyn Stablein

Bad Barbies

In the bathroom Tina keeps a bushel basket full of Barbies. The basket is piled high with naked, plastic dolls, their hair matted and disheveled. There must be thirty Barbies, one for each day of the month. Some of them belong to Tina's older sister. Two are mine. I babysit Tina in the afternoons when her mother works.

Every day Tina bathes the Barbies. She fills the tub with mint bubble bath, turns the bushel basket upside down over the water, then she slips into the foam with them. Together they make bubble boobs and bubble bras, bubble panties and bubble beards. Then Tina selects a Barbie to shampoo. She brusquely runs her fingers through the matted hair to untangle some of the strands, then splurts on clear golden baby shampoo from a plastic squeeze bottle that sits on the ledge of the tub. Back and forth Tina rubs the Barbie's hair between her hands like she's rolling out Playdough or making clay snakes. The Barbies never complain.

Tina is a big sister to the Barbies. They nestle alongside her in the tub, like a school of fish, a tribe of beauty queens, a pod of Barbies. During the shampoo the others float on their backs in the sudsy water staring at the bathroom ceiling, long hair spread out like seaweed. If they could sing, they'd sing about boys, pout love songs and hit parade tunes.

A wet Barbie is a bathing beauty, a water nymph like Esther Williams, mermaid of the chlorine pools whose feet twirl so effortlessly in the water, queen of the swan float, the lotus roll and scissor kicks.

Most days one of the Barbies acts up. Yesterday it was the Easter Barbie, who arrived all dressed up like a bridesmaid, lying in an Easter basket cushioned with a clump of green wax paper shredded into straw. A dozen red, blue, and yellow jelly bean Easter eggs and a scraggily blue feathered baby chick came with her in the straw basket. Tina stripped her for the bath, then left her clothes in a heap on the floor.

Tina makes rules to guide the Barbies. Still some misbehave. The Easter Barbie did something she shouldn't have done. Maybe she stepped out on the town without letting Tina know. Maybe she kissed a stranger.

There are problems with the other dolls, too, the pudgy babies who have trim circular holes the size of an eyedropper's for their mouths and trim circular holes where they pee after they drink from their bottles. For the babies Tina fills their bottles with water and nurses them. Then when the bottles are drained, she inspects and changes their diapers. She is both mother and father to these babies. When she bathes a baby in the sink, water seeps into the arm and leg joints and the baby's insides fill up. Then Tina squeezes the stomach so a stream of water and a gushing noise bursts from the hole. She replays this squirting again and again. The gushing stream is exciting and mysterious. When the babies are bad, they have temper tantrums. They cry and throw their bottles on the floor.

The Barbies are grown ups; they misbehave for different reasons. Barbies do not pee nor drink from toy bottles. A Barbie's skin is bright, a cross between wild cherry and strawberry ice cream, or the color of peach bubble gum. The hard plastic legs are shapely; the feet arch up, ready to slip into high-heeled slippers like Cinderella, ready to twirl, make pirouettes.

A Barbie is glamorous; she's a high fashion model who stars in Broadway theaters; she shops in department stores and boutiques. She is a city lady who knows how to primp and groom; she dresses as if she were going out on a date. She is ready for the man who watches her, who waits for her.

A Barbie never waits long. As soon as she dresses up, a man appears to escort her to the prom or movie. Barbies do not wear housecoats or aprons; they do not wear garden gloves or clothes to work in the garden. Barbies do not like to get their hands and clothes dirty. They wear rhinestone evening gowns, tennis outfits and sexy dresses with matching hats, stoles and heels in two colors: turquoise and hot pink.

The Easter Barbie was bad because she was lazy and stayed in bed too long; she didn't get up to go to work and was late for her rehearsal at the movie studio. She got into a fight with her boyfriend and hung the phone up on him when he called to ask her for a date. Maybe she also forgot to go to church. She was bad. Tina held the Easter Barbie in her hand and shook her.

"You are bad, Barbie!"

"I'm sorry."

"You slept in. You missed the rehearsal."

"I'm sorry."

"You kissed a man."

"I'm sorry."

"Your underwear is showing."

"I'll fix it."

"Hide your crack! Don't let a man see."

"I won't."

"You are bad, Barbie!" Tina turned her over and spanked her firmly but not too hard.

"No," Barbie pleaded. "Please don't. I won't do it again."

"Barbie, listen to me."

"I'm listening."

"Get to work! Faster! You're too slow."

"I'll hurry."

"Be home by ten o'clock!"

"I will."

"Listen up, Barbie. Pick up your clothes. Don't throw them everywhere."

"I'm listening. I promise."

The spanked Barbie settles right down. Sometimes Tina dresses her up afterwards; she'll comb out the hair, slip her into a sparkling, strapless evening gown and parade her around. After their daily communal soak in the tub, the other Barbies end up back in the bushel basket: a sprawling disarray of wet hair and lifeless bodies heaped together in a reckless, jumbled mass.

Wendy T. Dompieri

The Cut

Some people would consider my actions to be inexcusable, mean. I prefer to think of myself as a balancer of nature. Sure, there's some sarcasm in this evaluation, but we all have to look out for ourselves. Right?

Working as a beautician is hard work. First I had to borrow money to go to school. Then I had to work to pay the loan off. Guess most people know what it's like to begin at the bottom. You sweep the floors, follow everyone's orders, and shampoo dozens of heads until your fingers are numb. Day after day you do the basics with a smile until your big break comes. The break can come in several ways. Someone gets sick and you stand in for them; or it's prom time and there aren't enough beauticians in the world to prepare the sons and daughters of the town for their first formal.

Anyway it happens. It does eventually happen. You get your big break and you can start to be creative, to use what you've learned to earn real money. That's the best time, the scariest time. You have to prove yourself. If possible, you give each customer a little extra time. It's important that when they leave they look their best. It's even more important that they believe that it's you who's made them look their best.

And not only do you have to be a good stylist, you have to make the whole experience enjoyable. You have to size the customer up. Do they want to talk? Listen? How much? Do they have a definite idea of their style? Do you know enough to give them a new look? There's a lot to this business. It's not just coloring and styling. You have to know your customers and your business to build up a clientele.

For twenty years I've been helping people look their best. Twenty years. And as I said, this is hard work. The chemicals for instance. God only knows what they're doing to my insides. And all day you're on your feet. Being on your feet all day for twenty years does unkind things to a woman's legs. But that's beside the point. No, maybe that is the point.

All kinds of women come to where I work. Like yesterday. Yesterday Janice came in to have her hair trimmed. I've been doing Janice's hair for five years. She's a nice woman, pleasant to talk to, pleasant to look at. But she has a couple of flaws, physical flaws. You know, the kind most women have: protruding ears, a few veins on their legs, skin that's not so tight, body parts with too much fat.

I style her hair. We have a nice time together. You know, complaining about our husbands, worrying about our kids. The usual social stuff.

When I'm done, I tell her she looks wonderful. And she does. At the same time, we both know that she'll never again expose her arms unless she's on the beach. We both know that under that heavy makeup is an uneven skin tone. I look at her and I feel comfortable. Comfortable because I see balance. Nature has evened out all her parts.

Yesterday felt like a long day. By the time Linda came in, my ankles were already swollen. I was looking at myself in the mirror, wondering whether I should start to lighten my hair color.

As I stood looking in the mirror, Linda appeared beside me in the reflection. She was so striking, I was startled. A head taller than me; short dark hair.

"Hi, I'm Linda," she said in a perfectly modulated voice. "I'm Kristin's neighbor. She recommended you."

"Yes, of course. Let me give you to Jean to have your hair washed, then I'll be right with you," I replied, looking at her perfectly balanced features and clear skin.

How can I describe my thoughts when she returned and sat gracefully in the chair? I had watched her as she walked toward the sinks. She was slender without being thin, perfectly proportioned. I had hoped that on closer examination I would find something to fault her for: clumsy looking fingers, bony elbows, broken veins, cellulite. There was nothing. Even her hair needed the barest shaping.

"What can I do for you today?" I asked. I ask all my customers, just so they can feel they have control if that's what's important to them.

"I've been thinking of letting my hair grow to shoulder length," she replied. "Maybe you could just neaten up the front and trim off the dead ends in back."

I was aware I was becoming upset, agitated. Here before me was a perfect woman, and she wanted me, with all my imperfections, to make her even more perfect.

The first time I made "the cut" I had not planned the act. I remember it was about three years ago under similar circumstances. The woman was certainly as beautiful as Linda. As I said, I had not planned the act. It just seemed to happen. As I was trimming the hair towards the back of her head, I had made a cut that was very crude. At first it startled me to see the flaw in my work. I was almost afraid of the consequences of what would happen when the client discovered how careless I had been. Then a surprising thing happened. A feeling of deep satisfaction came over me. I knew I could cover the spot with what I'd learned in twenty years of experience. Some clever blow-drying, a good amount of gel, and the flaw would not be noticeable until later.

Now it was Linda's turn. I did my work, then covered the imperfection with blow-drying and gel.

"Thank you so much," Linda said as she left.

"Say hello to Kristin for me," I said with a smile.

In these past three years, I have perfected "the cut." As I said before, I'm a balancer of nature. Of course, the beautiful ones never come back.

As a friend, let me give you some advice. If you're an attractive woman, it's better to have a man do your hair. They'll be working to give you the best cut they know how. They want to please you enough that you'll be generous while tipping. They want you to come back.

Don't worry about me. There're enough average looking women in town to keep me going.

Dakota Lane

Sleeping with Jack

He is always leaving me. He's going off to his office or he's going off "to start my day." We never leave each other like normal people. Even when I'm at his house and I'm the one leaving, I have the sense that he's a real person having his real day and I'm the curled and wet thing scraped off that day. You might say it's a self-esteem problem, but I say it's something we create together. Or something that's bigger than both of us, completely out of our control.

One Sunday afternoon, in the first summer of our relationship, I was in my car in his parking lot with the sun streaming through my open window. The sky was dark blue and his parking lot was banked with walls of flowers. I felt like I was leaving Eden. Jack was in his car about to drive away, saying maybe I'll see you later. My car was facing down and his was facing up; our faces and arms hung out our windows and we were inches apart. I told him I felt lost inside. The only thing worse than feeling like that is what you experience at the moment of admitting to that feeling. The pitiful and loathsome inner child pops out, all big eyes and cuteness gone, just the whininess and snot nose remaining, all that sickening need leaking out of an aging adult body.

I sat there in my car, soaking in my emotional incontinence, biting my thumb, waiting for my fate.

Jack got a nice smile on his face and said he experienced the same kind of emptiness, only it wasn't about losing me, it was about all the beautiful women and exciting material things and glimpses of lifestyles he saw when he wandered the streets of the city alone at night. He went into that grabbier precursor to loss and became the Hungry Ghost of Buddhist lore, that big-stomached, big-headed, small throated creature who wants to eat the world but takes too much to swallow. He can never be full.

Sometimes just walking into the Barnes and Noble at night, he'd want not only all the clean and expensive books, but a beautiful wood-paneled and antique red leather library to stock them in, and not only the books and the library but the time to read the books and not only the time but a summer house to display the beachier books and not only the time and the beach and the books but the things within the books, the portraits of the children from Tibet, he wanted those children, he wanted their smiles and the genes from their parents which gave them those smiles so he could pass those genes on to his children which he wanted and not only did he want time and the children and the genes and the French provincial weathered southwestern tattooed Danish modern celebrity desert rock star intellectual sports gourmet ecologically sound everything of the everything that was in all those books, he wanted that thin, glossy haired, softly smiling, French-looking girl in the navy blue cotton shift, sitting across from him with a Japanese brush-painting book in her slender hands, her tan legs crossed and—standing now, lightly touching her girlfriend's shoulder, in that touch, the promise of 8,000 indescribably wonderful parties to which Jack will never be invited, he wants the French girl and her entire life, which he is sure takes place in orderly, spare splendor in some Little Italy loft and also internationally, with quietly ordered passports and never a scream or vaginal infection or request to fill her up, except on the most carnal level, which he would do most obligingly, in fact, right this second in the Barnes and Noble, bending her over the velvet rope by the cashiers, lifting her navy blue shift and parting her small, hard brown ass to reach the wet, sliced plum of her insides—but what about all the other asses in the world, the creamy cherry vanilla ones, the dimpled girlish ones, the black ones, the juicy, jiggly ones, take this one and the others won't be his, but since he hasn't taken this one yet and never will, leaving her and her ass is unbearable, since every scene she enters is like Bill Gate's fabled house, but instead of computers it is her very essence, or maybe her very ass, that triggers muted lights and delightful music and low, sweet laughter, preceding her entrances and following in her wake, every room and street and scene left barren and void in her absence. Still, Jack doesn't even follow her with his eyes after she leaves the table, although he might lift her Chinese brush-painting book after she is safely gone and briefly sniff at the smooth spine for her scent. He will leave the store without a purchase and wander the streets, vigilant in this fruitless pilgrimage, catching endless glimpses of the all-night movie, playing through golden lit windows and rooftop gardens, in the citrus shadows of the Korean market, through the opaque windows of passing limos and taxis, a movie starring all the things which will never be his and will never fill him up.

"There," he said. "That's how it is."

I could see Jack in that bookstore, with the blank-eyed air of a pervert or sage, looking pathologically self-contained. The natural human process of selection, rejection and commitment to a series of things and people had not been efficiently installed in his brain. Any fully embraced choice—that woman, that book, me—would automatically cut off an infinite of possibilities, with the absurd luck and finality of the speediest sperm lodging into an egg. Jack's life force was only in that wanting, never in the getting. The Hungry Ghost was Hungry not because he couldn't swallow but because he'd never helped himself to anything from the smorgasbord. Make no choice at all and leave the possibilities endless.

We looked at each other through our open car windows in his Technicolor parking lot.

Jack reached through his window and into mine and ran a finger from my eye down my cheek, where a tear would have streaked had I allowed one to get away from me. "I can't be more honest," he said.

I could address this honesty and engage him in conversation for a while—he never tired of my analysis of the many tricky and endearing aspects of his narcissistic character—or I could sidestep the whole show.

If I raised my chin a certain way, and adopted the air of a flirtatious stranger, perhaps he'd glimpse me as one of those dear, unreachable things. It was only in those moments, when he could trick himself into seeing me from an unfamiliar angle that he can feel desire for me and jump, with eyes half-closed, into my life for a moment.

"See ya," I said, the first to drive off, all the lack of closure and all the razoring pain worth it for that rearview glimpse of the admiration in his eyes. He could lick me up like bacon grease.

Two years later, we were pretty much in the same boat, although much kinder at times, and at other times much meaner. We had tried therapy, breaking up, no sex, just sex. I had tried to act like a man. I had tried to stop trying so hard and just let fate take us where it wanted, but unfortunately it usually took us to place like a Lake George gas station with me crying up against a phone pole while Jack stoically fed quarters into a machine then vigorously vacuumed out his jeep.

Our friends no longer liked us because all we could talk about were the minute details of our conflicts. We had become, as Jack told one of our therapists, a bad legend around town.

Sometimes we wouldn't see each other for weeks but that only made us stay on the telephone for hours. We spent most of our time together on the phone or at parties.

We're at a party I didn't want to go to. We're sitting around a bar. I see a fond look creep into Jack's eyes. I hate that fond look. I follow his gaze to a woman. Forty-something. Curly black hair. Short tight dress and the sort of sheer shiny black stockings he claims to hate. Once I wore stockings like those. I came downstairs all dressed up in those stockings and a short dress and he did this lip-pursing thing which I also hate and I waited for him to say how good I looked.

Finally I said: "What's the matter?"

He said, "You—" and then he looked away and shook his head, as if he couldn't bear to deal with the whole thing.

"What? What is it?"

"I thought you had a run, but it's—it's a shine."

"A what?" I looked my legs up and down. Not a run in sight. Just nice legs in ultra sheer silky black stockings. "Did you say a shine?"

He nodded, the lips pursed. Grim, almost.

"What's the matter, you don't like these kind of stockings?"

"Not really," he said.

"You think they look cheap or something? I mean tons of guys love it when I wear these kind of stockings."

"I'm sure they do."

"But you don't. You hate them."

"I didn't say I hated them." Jack hated using the word hate.

"But they make you sick."

"Oh please," said Jack. "Let's not bring this to a painful point."

I hated that expression. I hated that moment. And now I'm sitting at this bar hating the fond look on his face as he checks out this mop-headed chick with the shiny stockings. And she does have an incipient jowl. And she does have a glittery look in her eyes just for him.

I take off. She can't possibly be a threat, but I don't want to stand there and watch even the hint of anything transpire. I'm too weak for that sort of thing. I really am. I go up to our friend, a cute Filipino artist named Angel. I fling my arms around him and kiss his cheek. I've slept with him before.

"Angel," I say. "You look so good tonight. You want to go make out in the other room?"

I could see the mop-headed chick talking to Jack but I didn't really look again until one of Jack's buddies, a mournful-eyed opera singer, jabbed me in the arm and said:

"What's with Jack and Hertza? "

"What?"

"They're being so intense."

"Hertza? Is that really Hertza?" And here I'd been feeling sorry for the chick for four weeks straight in my exercise class because everyone was talking about how she was being cheated on by her husband, a little Napoleon-complexed man who was running around with a good-looking heiress. I'd never met the little man or the heiress or any of these folks, but any day now I knew I'd be making their acquaintance. This Hertza-in-person did not match my private-movie Hertza, a dumpy ethnicy peasanty simple soul, a thick-ankled Philip Roth muse, a large-assed R. Crumb girl. And in truth, I did not want to make out with Angel.

At the next party, Hertza was there again. Still wearing the curly do and the shiny black stockings. Now she was bending her ass over quite a bit while she looked for just the right dance music. Smiling and showing her teeth quite a bit to a certain dentist.

I still had no urge to do anything. I just looked at her jowls, her hair, the shiny stockings and I knew that she, poor soul, had no hope. She would never last a moment with that dentist. Not a second. Oh no, not her.

I kept my tortoise shell sunglasses and my leopard skin scarf on and I danced with myself in the mirror. I didn't care what any of them thought. I was a wild and sexual creature. Oh, that dentist was in for it. Oh, I was more than he could even hope to handle. I was young. She was old. I had no jowls. She had two. She was short and wore shiny stockings. I could go on.

But I didn't. I was quiet and cool and perfect. That was me. Perfectly drunk. But beautiful. No jowls. I did not possess the name of a car rental agency. I was not a desperate woman. I was not a desperate drunk. I was a punk rock drunk. I was a flying star. I was a hot commodity. She was not.

Did I mention that she was not, not in any way, was not! Was nothing!

He has a platonic fling with Hertza for a week and we break up for three weeks. He goes to Florida without me and while he is there I have a dream. I dream that I am awakened from sleep because Jack is in my house. I hear him enter my house through my sliding glass doors. I hear his heavy feet trying to walk gently across the wood floors. I hear him climb my stairs. I am still nearly paralyzed with sleep. I'm thinking—oh shit, I look horrible, he can't see me like this, all in bed, all a mess. But then he is leaning over my bed. It's two o' clock he says. He disappears. I wait a while before opening my eyes and turning to look at the digital clock, which reads 2:01.

One night we were on the phone for three hours. I lay on my bed with my ear on the phone and started saying less and less. I was getting tired. Hey, he said, don't fall asleep. I don't want to hang up, I said. I've got to go to sleep soon, he said. So go to sleep, I said. Just lay down. I am lying down, he said. Where, I said. On the chair. No, go on the couch, put the phone under your ear and lie on the couch. What are you saying, he said. Let's sleep together on the phone. Get outta here, he said. No, I'm serious. But no phone sex. What? he said. I didn't want to repeat it. I knew he heard what I said, he just wanted to be on the phone with someone hearing the words phone sex. I was too tired to repeat it but he kept saying what did you say? It doesn't matter, I said. It does matter, he said. No phone sex, I said. That's what I said. Oh, he said. Just go to sleep, I said. I can't, he said, I can't just leave the phone open all night, I'm expecting a call at five a.m. So I said, you have call waiting. We both laughed at that one. Come over and sleep with me, I said. What! he said. That's crazy, that's too crazy. No it isn't, I said. Come over and we'll sleep. No sex. Okay, he said, but we can't tell anyone. It's just too crazy. Can't tell anyone? I said. I don't think so. I'll tell whoever I want. Who are you afraid I'll tell? Your father? Your shrink? Okay, I'll come over, but I've got to be up at five a.m., I've got to leave exactly at five a.m. and I have to go right to sleep. That's fine, I said. Really? Yeah, really. Well, then I'm coming right over. Actually, I said, forget it. The whole thing was becoming too businesslike. Just the planning and the exact time and the stipulations about who not to tell, it was not the romantic, yearning-driven union a person might envision.

If I was going to have an ache filled I wanted it to be filled at the moment or as near as possible to the moment of the ache. You could savor it that way. One would think he felt the same way. Yearn. Fulfill. Need. Get. Not need, discuss it, negotiate and *then* fly into each other's arms.

What do you mean, you don't want me to come? I'm not sure, I said. Just say yes or no, he said. It's easy, yes or no. Okay, I said, no. But I was all set to come over, he said. Okay come. Okay then, I'm coming right now. We hung up.

I put a few heaps of clothes into the closet. I didn't bother with the bed. I went into the bathroom and saw my face and my straight smooth hair. I had no make-up on. I would be damned if I put my hair up. This was not about a night of fetishistic pleasures. And besides I was perfect. I had the perfect face. My face, if you can believe it, was at that moment perfect.

I decided to smoke a cigarette. I had my back to the door smoking like a fiend when he came into the house and walked up my stairs. It sounded just like the phantom of my dreams. The same steps. What if we hadn't had the call at all? What if I was truly losing it? But I didn't believe that for a second. I couldn't seem to put the cigarette out. I didn't know what to expect when I looked at him. I was already somewhat sorry he was there, but I'd have to go through with it. I was already thinking: he went to Florida without me. Without me. I was already rehashing a few other disturbing scenes, which I saw with increasing visual acuity, flashing through my head in sequence with bits of heightened gesture and dialogue like previews for horror movies. The moment on the Village Green at Christmas when his eyes locked with Hertza's and I was invisible. The moment in my kitchen when he brought his ex-wife and a bag of barbecued chicken wings to my roast chicken dinner. I was going through this little movie or at least sitting down in the dingy theatre of my mind, putting my feet up on the chair and getting my popcorn settled, when he walked in and stood for a while before saying:

Hello?

I gave him a winning smile. Hi!

He took off his pants and got into bed.

I got in beside him and turned off the light.

Good night! I said, and rolled to my side, my back to him. I really thought I might fall asleep. He put his arm around me. You can sleep? he said. Hmmm, I said. I really thought I could, if I could just slip into the gap before any funny business came up. The room was bright. The moon was shouting.

We lay there for a while. I didn't want to talk about anything. I didn't want any physical contact. I wanted to hear his breathing and echo his rhythm so I could fall asleep. Of course I knew that he was debating something inside his head. I could feel it. He might grab me, I thought. And then he did.

He pulled me to him hard. I didn't mind that. But I didn't want any more. Come here, he said and I let him turn me so I was pressed up against him. His breath smelled like strong coffee. It wasn't so bad. But he had this light perfumey smell to his hair and sweatshirt. It was a reminder of our being apart, this new smell like a woman's cheap perfume or a fruity shampoo or something he might have picked up in a Florida mall. But I didn't want to complain. It was never my style to complain at such fragile moments.

We still said nothing. And then he suddenly pulled my pajama pants down and pulled my shirt up and let his hands roam all around my body. It was kind of an Aha! move—like see what I can do. Or let's see what you're hiding under there, did you fuck someone else. I didn't mind it too much either, in fact it was quite a thrill to feel such passion coming from him, and a big hard-on pressed around my stomach, but still I didn't want this to turn into sex. I felt a real pull to have sex, but I also heard a scream in my head, or a whine, a long whine saying: what about the perfect childhood and the money? What about *that*, huh? I was on the sex list but not the Florida list. I was on the cunnilingus list but not on the perfect ideal woman list. I didn't even want to kiss him, but he was saying Come on now, or Come here, or something so I slightly kissed him back. He had a big open coffee smelling mouth.

I put my hands on the back of Jack's neck and he sighed. He needed to be touched so much. He needed affection. I took my hands away. I could not feel affection. He'd gone to Florida without me. Too many things had happened or not happened.

He turned his back after a while. I didn't like that too much. He had me sleep with my stomach against his back. I didn't like it but I thought I'd try it. We lay there for a while. I could see the black bare branches out the window and clouds lit up in the night sky. I wouldn't have been surprised to see a UFO. After a while he lay on his back. I stared at the sky. I would have *loved* to see a UFO. To say Look! and both of us to see that thing zip a silvery staggered path in the night.

I went up on my elbow and tried to see his face. I could see the face but couldn't tell if his eyes were open. He never had the need to stare at me. Or maybe he did, but I never saw it. To be fair, I never had the need to stare at him that much. But at least I had the need to feel the need. I wondered if he opened his eyes if he would see my perfect face or if the light was just right to give me a ghoulish, prematurely lined face. Or if he could ever look at me and see the lines and the strangeness and still feel an overwhelming love.

Neither of us was contented. Now and then I'd move, closer to him, but in an innocent way, and he once said: You rascal.

What a strange thing to say. Who was this man?

He pulled me to him again. I can't sleep, he said. My body won't let me sleep. Your body feels so good. I felt pleasure at this, pure pleasure at his words and then a little voice: Your *body*? Why not *me*? Why don't *I* feel good? Shut up, I thought.

What did Deepak say about this, about finding the negative in things? Did Deepak say that? Oh, be willing to tell yourself that you don't know the whole picture. Be willing to tell yourself that you're projecting. That your lover is only giving you the very lesson you need to learn. What if he hits you in the face, Deepak? Are you really hitting *yourself* in the face? Are you supposed to thank him? But Jack was not hitting me in the face. He was saying my body felt good. Easy for him to say after he'd been to Florida, and had some color and sun and an eyeball full of tropical flowers and palm trees. Easy for him to say after he's sat down and composed me write off the list. Hmm, let me see here—no sirree, she seems to be coming up a little short. She's missing just two qualities, but they're very important qualities in a woman, in fact, essential: happy childhood and loads of dough. Shut up, I told myself, his going there was not an attack on me. His list is just showing me what I'm missing. Okay, I'll change, I promise—god darn it, I'll go out and git myself a happy childhood right this very instant, I will. He can't help it if he's scared and wants to think he wants someone who's completely content and perfect. Don't see it in the worst possible light. *Oh shut up shut up.*

I haven't been this way in years, Jack said. You know me, I can always fall asleep. It's the moon, I said. No, I drank a pot of coffee, he said. But you always drink coffee and sleep, I said. This time I can't, he said. Did you ever think it's your feelings that are keeping you awake, I said, that it's your feelings and your just feeling them in your penis? I know it's my feelings, he said. I'm not just feeling them in my penis. I didn't ask him to elaborate. What time is it? he said. I told him it was two. Shit, he groaned. I feel like I just did a whole gram. I know, I said. I can't sleep either. Am I keeping you up?

No, he said. We lay there for minutes, another half an hour. He said my name in a groan. He never does that. I had no feeling to help him. Do you want to leave? Please, go if you want, I said. No I just want to sleep, he said. I want to sleep too, I said. Then do, he said. Sleep. I looked at the sky. It was almost three. I put my arms around him and he said, I know you didn't invite me here to spend the night and have sex with you. I know you didn't plan on having sex. That's true I said. But why do you keep saying sex? You don't usually say that. Well, it's what you said, he said. You said no sex. Right, I said.

I put both my legs over his. What are you doing? he said, not annoyed but put my legs off his. I just can't have anything heavy on me. Are you saying my legs are heavy? Let's get his straight, he said, I am not saying your legs are heavy. I just can't sleep like that. Here. He arranged things so our legs made a sandwich with only my ankle on top of his, or something like that, my limbs were too dead to know who they were and where they were and who they were with and in precisely what arrangement.

I remembered the pain of the week without him. I felt his desire to be with me, to make me feel better. I know he's good. I'm disturbed but I still have this soul thing. I put my arms around him and slid them down his back. I was too tired to give him a massage. But I played with his ass for a while as if it were an object having nothing to do with a human, a fun pliable toy I found in my hands on the beach. He might have been annoyed or turned on or annoyed that he wasn't being turned on but he just allowed me this play without any sort of intervention or guidance.

He took my hands after a while and held them against his chest... and some minutes later I woke, realizing I had slept. There was such beauty in that, realizing that my hands had put themselves to sleep on his chest and my brain had followed. There was no beauty in seeing the clock. 4:50. The alarm went off at five. He got up and said Bye baby, I gotta go. Bye I said, trying to smile. He kissed my cheek. Or my mouth. Or my head. Or perhaps didn't kiss me at all. I was too tired for anything to make an impression except for the sound of his feet going down the stairs, his car running outside and then the engine going away, down the street.

I stared out at the whitening sky until I heard nothing and could draw his pillow close to me and fall back asleep.

Phillip P Levine

✷

Soon

The day. The day is light. And the day is long and has many rooms between the hours. The day also travels a long arc up and up and then back down again from middle, and a Calculus can count the length and width and area beneath this curve and tell us this place is large and has room for many things, many that we know, and many more still. There is a room for joy with her large funny hat, that bounces as she bounces, with laughter or something like it. And sadness too, can have a room, she who likes to sleep, to take naps in the afternoon between top and shadow.

And today is also a place I know and go to as if returning, and so I know there is a point or place or time for you and me along this curve of day, a place by the fire, where we can burn all our old stories of loss and failure and warm our feet while we do it, because this fire is warm and soothes. And this fire is also hot and dances. And I see it in your eyes. And I know it is in mine. And by this fire I can watch your fingers curl and uncurl and think perhaps they wish to touch. And I can feel mine curl and uncurl too, even as I think to hold them still. But they will not, as they have ten hearts and minds and desires of their own and wish to find their mates in yours.

So one by one to five then ten they arch across the spaces there between us, that is, the spaces between mine and yours and all that could be ours, like your ten with their ten, their hearts and minds and desires and all the same as all of mine and all that dances there in the light of this fire. And soon together ten and ten close and open. Open and close together again. And soon beads of moisture gather there in their folding and, glistening, collect the light.

Then I risk to think they will be sweet when tasted, but it is to be waited for like dessert. For is not waiting the sweetest taste of all?, for what is it but anticipation that brings a mouth to water?, that brings the tongue to swelling, that purses lips and opens eyes to wide and wider still. So I am feasting in this waiting, and if we share this waiting, then so we share a feasting. And in this way a feast is made.

And by this, my heart is quickened, and soon it also pauses. And soon again quickens and soon again pauses. And soon this hardens and soon this softens, and soon between the beating, and between the pausing, and between the hard, and between the soft, soon there would be touching, yes soon. Yes soon there will be touching, and yes soon there will be touched, and soon I will, yes soon you will, yes soon we will. Yes. Soon. Soon.

Soon.

Valerie Wacks

What Simon Doesn't Say

Simon had always been a quiet child, but by the age of six, he stopped speaking altogether. His mother took him to a series of specialists, who after probing, poking, X-rays, CAT scans and MRI's, determined the problem was not physical. Simon already knew this, but he didn't say anything. He thought there were too many people in the world and they all made too much noise. He had decided to use his mouth for essentials only: eating and drinking and the occasional yawn.

Now it was summer and Simon spent his days beneath an oak tree in the corner of their small back yard. He lay on his back under the tree and looked up at the spots of blue sky between the dark branches and green leaves. He memorized the shapes of these spaces and gave the larger ones names like Blue Dog, Fox Face and Hairy Spider. He marked the place where he rested his head with a small stone. Each day he'd lie down on the scruffy dirt and grass in the same position, and silently greet his familiar spots. When the wind blew, the shapes would disappear into ripples of light and dark. Simon named this pattern River-tree and tried to follow the dapples' movements until he felt dizzy and had to close his eyes.

His mother was very busy. She worked all day and took classes at night.

"I'm sorry to leave you alone so much," she said one evening over their dinner of take-home Chinese food. Simon sat and picked the water chestnuts out of his chicken chow mein.

"I have to think about our future. Who knows how long your dad will keep up the support payments, and then what would happen?" She poked at a piece of bright orange shrimp, then stabbed a chunk of pineapple with one chopstick and thrust it into her mouth. She bared her teeth and drew the empty chopstick out slowly, stopping to chew on the chopstick tip. The pineapple pouched out her cheek like a chipmunk's.

Simon smiled and tried to spear a water chestnut with his chopstick, but it skittered onto the tabletop. He glanced at his mother. She was staring out the kitchen window, swallowing and frowning and drumming on the edge of her plate with her chopsticks. He picked up his fork and ate some rice.

"Are you sure you don't want to go to summer camp, Simon? It's not too late to sign up." She looked over for his response.

Simon swallowed his mouthful of rice and shook his head, no.

"Just as well," she said. "After all those doctor bills and my tuition, we don't have much money left. Why did I let your dad talk me out of finishing school when we got married? Why did I marry that creep in the first place? Why do I still bother talking about him?" She shook her head and pushed back her plate and stood up from the table.

"At least I have you," she said and tousled his hair. Her hand was warm and smelled of soy sauce. "Do you mind clearing up? I've got to run to class. Just call me the computer whiz kid, inputting our way to financial security if not fortune. Remember, Mrs. Beezle is right next door if you need anything."

Simon did not mind clearing up. It was one of his jobs, like staying in the yard during the day, and making sure all the doors were locked at night before he went to bed. His mom had taught him how to scrape the plates clean, rinse them and stack them in the dishwasher. He did this now, climbing on a little footstool by the sink so he could reach the faucets. Then he put the leftover cartons of food in the refrigerator, climbed back up on the stool, wet a sponge and wiped the counters clean, and then wiped off the kitchen table.

He went back into the yard and sat under the oak tree, watching the sunset paint colors in the sky. As the sky quieted and crickets began to chirp, he watched the flicker of fireflies in the gathering dusk. He tried not to blink so he could follow each firefly and catch every flash of golden light. He called this game See-all and played until his eyes watered. Then he blinked three times and began again.

"Cat still got your tongue, Simon?" Mrs. Beezle called. Simon sat up and watched her approach, shuffling through her yard to his, bringing his lunch as she did every day at noon.

"We've got bologna and cheese and don't pick out the lettuce. A growing boy needs his greens."

Simon stared down at the pink terrycloth slippers, the white puffy ankles traced with blue veins. With a grunt, she squatted down next to him, smelling of sweat and flowery talc. Simon practiced his blank face.

"Why so serious, young man?" She said. "You know, your mom looks prettier every day. It's been over a year since your daddy left and now she's polishing her nails and put a perm in her hair. Maybe someday soon, you'll have a new daddy. Won't that be nice?"

Simon stared down at his hands. Mrs. Beezle sighed and hauled herself back up. "Okay, honey. Maybe tomorrow you'll feel like talking," she said. She said this every day. He heard her shuffle away and soon the familiar sounds of afternoon soaps wafted into his yard on the muggy summer air.

Simon opened his sandwich on its paper plate. He removed a yellow square of cheese, folded it in half, then in quarters, broke each quarter in half and ate them one at a time. Next he peeled the skin off the edge of the bologna, dangled it above his mouth like a skinny worm and slurped it through his lips like a strand of spaghetti. He rolled the two skinless circles of bologna into tubes and ate them with quick neat bites. He licked the mayonnaise off the white bread and ate the bread except for the crusts. Then, using a stick, he dug a shallow hole in the dirt by the chainlink fence that bounded the back of their property. He put the lettuce in the hole and covered it up. Maybe it would grow.

He carried the paper plate and bread crusts into the kitchen and threw them in the trash. He poured himself a glass of apple juice without spilling any, drank it, climbed up on the footstool and rinsed out his glass, then set it upside-down in the dishdrainer.

Lunch taken care of, he resettled under the oak tree. The sky was cloudy. Blue Dog had turned into Grey Dog. Simon lay on his back and closed his eyes. He remembered the night his father left.

He had been awakened by loud angry voices from his parents' bedroom. He needed to go to the bathroom, but he knew on nights like this, he was supposed to stay in his room. He tried to hear what they were saying. Were they fighting about him? His dad boomed like thunder and his mom's voice was frantic and high. Then he tried not to listen and pulled the covers over his head. But it was too dark and stuffy and he poked his head back out. His dad's voice got louder and the words flew faster. His mom's voice rose too. Now he could understand what she was saying. She was screaming a dirty word.

Suddenly there was a loud crash and the sound of breaking glass. His mom was silent now. He heard his dad storm into the hallway. Simon quickly closed his eyes and pretended to be asleep. He heard the front door open and slam closed. He heard his dad's car pull out of the driveway. Then it was quiet except for the sound of crickets chirping outside of his bedroom window. A slight breeze fluttered the curtains.

He got out of bed and walked down the hall to his parents' room. He stood by the door, but his mom did not see him. He walked into the room. She was sitting on the floor surrounded by shards of glass from the shattered dresser mirror. She was crying. He looked down and saw pieces of himself and his mother reflected in the jagged fragments: a patch of his blue pajamas, a bit of her pink tee shirt, random reflections of his and her flesh. It looked like a jigsaw puzzle with the pieces all mixed up.

His mom looked at him with swollen red eyes. "Don't touch the glass and don't look at me. Just go back to your room," she said.

The next day he saw her standing by the low row of hedges that separated his yard from the Beezle's, talking to Mrs. Beezle in low rapid tones. "Better the mirror than your face, honey," he heard Mrs. Beezle say.

Simon opened his eyes and stared up at the tree and the cloudy sky. He practiced See-all until the greens and greys smeared together, and thin tears leaked from the sides of his eyes. Then he closed his eyes again.

The air was heavy and still. Simon felt the earth press up against his back and felt the blades of grass prickling his skin. He felt ants crawling up his bare arms and legs. He held perfectly still and breathed, down into the ground and up into the air, down into the ground and up into the air. Simon became a mound of earth, a small mountain for the ants to explore.

"I'm home, Simon. Come inside, I've got something to show you." Simon sat up and saw his mother at the kitchen window, her face blurred by the screen.

"Your class pictures finally came in the mail today," she said as he walked in. Simon rubbed his eyes with his fists. His mother pulled a photograph out of a large manila envelope and placed it on the kitchen table.

"Not a bad likeness," she said. "But you should've combed your hair before it was taken. Didn't the photographer say anything?"

Simon shook his head and squinted at the picture. He tried to figure out which of the little boys was him. It had been a long time since he'd looked in a mirror and now, he didn't know how to recognize himself. He scanned the five rows of children in the photograph and looked for a boy with messy hair. Several fit that description.

"I ordered three extra copies," his mother said. "One for Mrs. Beezle, one to mail to grandmom and one to put on my desk at work. At least I have something to show for myself."

She sounded angry. Was she angry at him? Simon licked his hand and tried to smooth down his hair. He glanced up at his mom, but she had turned towards the refrigerator. He looked back at the rows of little faces. Perhaps, if he could name all the faces of the other boys in his class, the one left over would be him. But that would be a stupid and boring game. Simon put the photograph back in its manila envelope.

Several days later, he was out in the backyard. It was a hot afternoon and his seventh birthday. For lunch, along with a tuna salad sandwich, Mrs. Beezle brought him a cupcake with chocolate icing. He licked the icing off the cupcake, but the cake itself was tasteless and dry. He dug a hole in the yard and buried the cake, marking the spot with a small stone. Maybe it would rain and the cupcake would grow moist baby cupcakes.

Simon felt restless and decided to play the footstep game. He walked by the chainlink fence from one end of the yard to the other, clasping his hands behind him and gazing straight ahead. He silently counted each footstep. There were two variations to this game. In one, Simon tried to take the exact same number of steps each trip up and back. In the other, Simon just kept counting his footsteps as he kept walking. He knew how to count very high. When he forgot and lost track of the numbers, he had to start over at one again. Today, Simon opted for the latter version and added a bonus. If he could walk and count up to 500 three times in a row without losing his place, he could spray himself with the garden hose to cool off, and then begin the game again.

"Your clothes are all wet," his mother said when she got home from work. "You know I've asked you to change into a bathing suit before going under the hose."

Simon looked down at the ground and scuffed at a tuft of grass with his toes.

"Well, never mind," she said. "Come on inside. Your dad sent a birthday gift for you along with his support payment. Let's go in and check it out. And don't forget to wipe your feet."

Simon followed her into the kitchen. There was a package on the table, wrapped in brown paper and tied with a string. His mom cut the string with a knife. "You can open it now, but be careful. It's marked fragile."

He opened the paper along the taped edges and drew out a double-paned glass rectangle with a wooden frame. Dirt was sandwiched between the glass panes, crisscrossed by tunnels in which he could view the frantic activity of a colony of ants.

"An ant farm," his mother exclaimed. "As if we didn't have enough bugs around here in the summer. And he didn't even bother with a card."

Simon pointed to a small piece of colored construction paper taped to the corner of the ant farm.

"That says 'Old-fashioned Formicary. Handmade in Vermont'. It's not a note from your dad."

His mother stood by the kitchen table, sighed and tousled his hair. "Listen Simon, I've got to go out now. Exams are next week and I'm meeting a friend to go over some homework before class. I left pizza for you on the counter, your favorite with sausage. When I get home later tonight, we'll invite Mrs. Beezle over for ice-cream and cake, and celebrate your birthday for real. Okay?"

Simon nodded without looking up.

"And listen, play with that thing outside, okay? I don't want any ants escaping into the kitchen."

After she left, Simon walked over and poked at the pizza. It was lukewarm. He wasn't hungry anyway. He picked up the ant farm, went out into the backyard and sat down under the oak tree.

Ant sandwich. Formicary. He tasted the new word silently. He peered into one glass wall and saw his face reflected dimly against the dirt and scurrying columns of ants. He placed the ant farm flat on the ground, picked up a rock and hammered at it until the glass shattered. Then he lay on his back on the ground.

He felt the tickling of grass and ants on his body, felt the softness of the dirt and the sharpness of the shards of broken glass.

He lay motionless beneath the tree for a long time with his eyes open wide to the early evening sky. The wind blew Rivertree, but Simon didn't name it. He had turned into an ant and crawled into his own ear.

Lucy Hayden

✷

Blaze

I could see at the edge of the woods a slash of blaze orange and, against the dark gray of the woods, two darker shapes. The leaves were gone and the ground brown. The orange moved from right to left, and I watched it with a thought close to praying, a melancholy wish that my son would always be safe. Lately this thought comes often. James knew he should be home for dinner soon, but still I kept an eye on the orange slash as I worked.

In my dream the night before, the dog, Angus, had cried outside the front door, and when I opened it, I saw a pack of wild hounds behind him, a voracious, unpredictable threat, moving toward me like a tidal wave. In the dream, I just barely pulled him into the house before slamming the door on the pack. Their teeth were bared at me, their eyes hard and predatory. When I woke, I knew with certainty that James was the dog and that the pack was what was to come.

From our house, I can see three mountain ranges: the Catskills to the west, the Berkshires to the north, the Housatonic range to the east. We live on a crest in the Taconic range. There is no town, and many roads are unpaved. In the spring we roll away the rocks that the frost has heaved into the field. Our well is our survival.

This backwoods life is both antisocial and civilized, a contradiction I no longer worry about. A neighbor once said to me, in reference to some scandal in the city, "I'm so glad we don't have a government," which about sums up how many people here feel. James has been raised here, and he has never known anything else. He goes to school on the bus, he comes home again, and the larger world waits for him down in the valley and away.

I saw the orange slash move off into the woods. A truck passed on the road. As in every November dusk, pick-up trucks were prowling the dirt roads, looking for unposted or unwatched woodland. There are many things you don't know about America if you grow up in the city. Things I have learned: One, everyone has a gun. Two, private property is a relative concept. Three, a lot of people still kill their own food. You see where my mind was leading.

I skipped downstairs and quickly threw on an old waxed-cotton jacket, wrecked and uninsulated. Leather gloves were in the pocket, and I pulled them on. Out the window I did not see the orange. I left the back door unlocked and stepped into the wind.

"James! James! Dinner time!" I cupped my hands around my mouth in a useless attempt to call him. Shouting into a 20-knot wind at someone four hundred yards away, over an open field and into the woods, is as good as nothing. I started quickly down the hill toward where the orange had disappeared. James wore the little strip of blaze-orange fleece around his waist at my insistence. Because we live on a mountain, in a place we like to call Old Nowhere, James has yet to cross a street unattended, but he's wandered the woods alone for years. Today he was with Angus, a silly, meandering dog whose inclinations tend more to napping than to chasing rabbits.

When I reached the edge of the woods, I saw the deer trail they had probably taken. It didn't make me any happier. Again I called into the woods, "James? Angus! Come back!" Nothing but the wind and the cold came back. I followed the path to where it became wet and then turned up the hill. The ground was slippery and the daylight fading fast, with none of the lingering halflight of summer. I quickened my pace climbing the hill, thinking of things I shouldn't.

Near the top of the hill, I thought I heard voices and called out once more. Again, nothing. In the direction of the road I heard an engine turn over. It was dark. I turned back toward the house. Going downhill, the unseen branches slapped my face and wet logs turned underfoot. James is smarter than this, I thought. James knows the woods, and he knows the dangers. He's been told. I thought of the thin strip of orange that stands between him and a gun. I thought of the dog and how far James might go. Something small moved in the dark. My tights tore on the brambles. My ankle twisted on a rock. Down the hill, through the wet, through the narrow trail, up the field, to the house.

The kitchen lights were on. Inside, James was standing at the counter filling the kettle, his cheeks and nose red with cold, his face happy and bright. "I saw the hunter again, Mom," he said. "He's the guy who put the roof on the barn, remember? He's a really nice guy. He was up in that old deer stand and we had a chat." I stared at him, his happy face, his body small and fragile. James, who talks to everyone. And I thought of the world outside, waiting.

Brent Robison

In the Waiting Room

Emily looks at the young woman's mouth as she speaks. "...anonymous passerby," she seems to be saying.

Or "enormous pecan pie." Emily can't really be sure.

The young woman is dressed in olive coveralls. Her hands are freckled and strong. She has a guileless Dorothy Hamill haircut. The young woman is an Emergency Medical Technician. Emily suddenly imagines her rimmed by headlights, waltzing tenderly with a broken body at a highway's edge in the middle of the night. Her upper lip and cheeks are covered with very fine golden hair that catches, in hypnotic rhythm as she speaks, the cold glow of the waiting-room fluorescents.

Emily's husband Sammy is listening intently. His stare is at once both focused and glazed. He asks something that just maybe could be "Is celestial radiance a particle or a wave?" But probably not.

Emily can't listen. Emily saw the glance between the young woman and the ER surgeon. The surgeon had three pinhead-size spots of blood on his white smock, arranged in perfect proportion: Las Vegas, Los Angeles, Lake Tahoe. He needed a shave. His jaw reminded Emily of Mount Saint Helens after the blast. "Cuppa mud, anyone?" he had said a few minutes ago, poking his head in the door. Mount Saint Helens cracked, a little one-sided grin. The surgeon had come directly from the operating room to speak to them in person. His eyelids were lined in red.

Sammy said, "No, thanks." He didn't see the glance. Or any glance, ever. He never had. He is congenitally glance-blind, Emily is sure. If there is a gene for the perception of interpersonal subtleties, Sammy's dim ancestors misplaced theirs somewhere along the trail from the cave to the waterhole.

Sammy would never understand why she is thinking now, as she does so often, of the waterfall in Colorado. She was six months along then, almost twenty years ago. She and Sammy had taken off all their clothes and were clenched in a kiss under the freezing shower when a Japanese family appeared on the ledge below and stood in a neat row, big to little, four mannequins with Nikons to their eyes. Emily and Sam bowed in a grand theatrical manner, all wet goosebumps and shriveled flesh, and ran for their clothes. Even now, not a month goes by that she doesn't reflect on this: her anonymous pallid self, totally revealed, heavy breasts and rounded belly and dark pubic hair all dripping, pasted neatly in four plastic photo albums somewhere in Tokyo.

Emily knows that Sammy, in his serious voice, the voice that goes with his silvering temples, the voice that she kids him about, will tell her tomorrow. He'll tell her of the anonymous passerby, the one who called the ambulance. Then Emily can dutifully research the person's name. She can send a pretty thank-you note, as if this were a wedding. In a flowery script on embossed paper: "Many thanks for passing that deserted off-ramp at 2 a.m. this past Saturday...." or "Our sincere gratitude for your timely presence at the twisted wreck on I-15...." Maybe flowers would be appropriate. The delicate day lilies along the picket fence would make a perfect bouquet; but no, they won't be up until June, and that's if the deer don't eat them first.

What is post-trauma etiquette? Is there a book at Barnes and Noble?

Later, Emily is thinking. It can be done later, but here in the waiting room, there is no later. There is only this: a glance between the surgeon and the EMT. Was it a quick glance, or did it linger? Could it have been merely a random flick of the eyes? Was it simply a nonverbal hello, a nod to a colleague? Or was it as heavy with meaning as was her body that one and only time, for those few months, years ago? Those months that led to a birth, that led, eventually, to this place, on this night?

Now, the young blond EMT and the rough-jawed surgeon and her own dear, silly Sammy look at each other and gravely nod and move their lips in a slow ridiculous pantomime. They are saying something about the person in the room just down the hall. Or are they speaking of the weather?

It all recedes, because right now, Emily remembers the afternoon. Earlier today—or was it yesterday?—when that quick March storm blew through.

"Yo, mamacita mi amor, 'm outta here." Matthew had entered the kitchen with half a bagel in his mouth, swinging a knapsack over his shoulder.

"OK sweetie, see ya." Emily didn't ask; she knew already: Friday afternoon, design class, then to his friend Jack's house, maybe some band rehearsal, maybe some cruising and partying until late.

A gust of wind banged the screen door. She glanced up from the dishes in the sink; Matthew barely paused on his way out. He tossed back his long front lock. "Peesh 'n' lerve." Silver glinted from multiple earrings.

"Peesh 'n' lerve to you too." She smiled, eyes back on the soapy dishes.

He backed out of the driveway with a grin and a wave. She waved in return, sponge in glove, flinging soapsuds across the window with something like abandon. *Faux-abandon, maybe,* she had thought with a chuckle.

As her son's old green Beetle disappeared over the hill, Emily had stared at the construction site next door. Soon there would be a concrete parking garage for a new condo complex, where once had stood a row of sturdy brick bungalows like her own. It had become an alien landscape. Charcoal clouds boiled in from the west, weeds bent low in the wind, and the first drops began to splatter the ground. Emily stood still and silent at her kitchen window. As she watched in the iron-gray light, across the heaps of earth, across the rubble of brick and broken foundations and the tangled, rusted re-bar, came a daisy-yellow umbrella, open, twirled by chance gusts, with a float, a leap, a dip, a tumble, dancing a slow motion ballet before the storm.

Lanette Fisher-Hertz

Quitting

I started smoking again at the age of thirty-eight at a bachelorette party in a male strip club in Wildwood. Whenever I try to trace my way back, that first drag is the moment I remember.

A restless, unfocused desire was already pulling at me, tightening the muscles in my face and throat, the night my sister-in-law, Paula, drove us to that club. While she maneuvered her Astro mini-van down I-5, I leaned my head out of the van window, squinting into the warm wind. The closer we got to Wildwood, the more cigarette billboards I saw. I hadn't smoked since I'd married Paula's brother, Ben, fifteen years earlier, but I could almost taste the one I planned to have that night.

"Carol, Jesus, how did you talk me into this?" Paula asked, shaking her head as she parked beneath giant neon outlines of men's bodies.

"It's good to do something different once in a while," I assured her, even though I couldn't remember the last time I had.

We had no trouble spotting our party of women in the back, mostly teachers at the elementary school where I was the K-5 librarian. As soon as we sat down, I saw Janet, the bride-to-be, smoking a long brown cigarette.

"What's this?" I asked, picking up the pack of Mores next to her drink.

"I figure this is my last night to try everything," she said. She shrugged and sucked in some smoke, made a face. "I don't even like them anymore, so this is more nostalgic than anything else."

"Perfect," I said. "I'm feeling nostalgic, too."

By the time the DJ started talking to the crowd, most of us were buzzed on cheap champagne and giddy with nervous laughter. I made myself wait, the way I did with my popcorn at the movies, not tasting any until the opening credits were done. I slipped a cigarette out of Janet's pack, held it between my fingers for a moment—then turned away from Paula's watchful eye. Holding the lighter to the tip, I closed my eyes and assured myself I could contain the smoking to just this one night. My first draw was dizzying and evocative; I felt eighteen, high and stupid all over again.

The dancers were sexier than I'd anticipated. They swaggered out in uniforms and costumes—cowboys, Indians, policemen—like a parody of the Village People, but genuinely seductive anyway. The music pounded against our dampening bodies. We screamed like girls, slid dollars into their g-strings, fell still and breathy when they held our faces or stared into our eyes.

Afterward, in a diner, gobbling down piles of food in an effort to satisfy the desires the dancers had evoked, we turned confessional.

"Do you think that last dancer had a sock in there?" asked Janet. "No one is that big, right?"

We howled raucously at our memory of The Italian Stallion, who had a comically long, leather-clad bulge that he never uncovered.

"I wouldn't want it that big!" I said. "But I wouldn't mind it that slow."

In the Stallion's final routine, he chose one of the oldest women there, a solid-boned woman with a long, steel-colored braid and giant hoop earrings, and caressed her everywhere. He brushed his hands across her forehead, ran finger traces up and down her throat, slid his wide hands around her shoulders, played teasingly up her calves, pressed his palms lightly inside her thighs, traced his breath in a column down her spine—all while he danced around her, gazing adoringly at her, never touching the rest of his body against her. Even though it was campy, the woman responded as if she'd been hypnotized, raising herself toward him, her chest pushed outward, her breathing shallow enough that we could all see for ourselves the effect he was having on her.

There was a collective sigh as we all thought about him for a moment, several of us pushing back from the table and lighting up after-meal smokes. I'd bought my own pack by then from the club's vending machine.

I thought of the lovemaking I'd had with Ben that morning, pressed between the navy-blue sheets in case the girls ran in, no time for foreplay, no chance for me to experience the orgasm he was able to have within minutes. I hadn't even had time to pleasure myself before we had to jump up and shower, get the kids to the bus, get to our jobs.

Paula spoke, almost shyly, but boasting, too: "Actually, Shane makes love like that," she said. We all stared at her.

"With a sock in there?" Janet asked, cracking us all up again.

"No, really," Paula said, "Like I imagine a woman would, actually, very slowly. He was unlike any other man I'd ever been with—that's why I married him. He loves to touch, everywhere, real slow. Sometimes he doesn't even go in, just spends hours driving me crazy. I actually pass out sometimes."

We sat up straighter. This was sobering news—that there could be a husband like that. Paula and Shane had been married thirteen years. What did Paula's revelation mean about our own marriages? Even Janet, the not-yet-newlywed, stared, open-mouthed, in a way that told us her groom-to-be wasn't that patient, either.

"When do you find time?" I asked, awed, suddenly imagining Shane's long, pale fingers playing over Paula's generous, dark body...lingering for hours. I closed my eyes and tried to shake the image away.

"Well, you live next door, so you know we don't watch much TV," she said, laughing, pushing her thick hair out of her face. Then, embarrassed, she added: "I mean, it's not that often, just a few times a week."

"A few times a week!" several of us shouted in unison, indignant. By now the jealousy was palpable, and I could see Paula regretted having spoken.

The rest of us began confessing how long it had been in our marriages since we'd last had sex. More than a year for one woman. Months for several. The average seemed to be once a week, with most of us waiting for Saturday nights if we wanted anything longer than a ten-minute turn-around time. My own morning quickie had been an anomaly; my husband and I usually made love every week or two, almost always at night—after the girls were in bed and the bills paid and the dishes and laundry put away. When Ben helped, I knew he was interested.

Paula stopped talking, went back to her eggs and toast. Close as we were, she had never talked to me about her sex life before—perhaps because she didn't want to hear any details about my sex with her brother. Not that I would have been able to shock her. I'd assumed she and Shane enjoyed the same comfortable, routine affection I had with Ben; I was struck dumb imagining her hours of passion under Shane's patient attentions.

After that night, I started craving cigarettes more than I had in years—and giving in to the desire. I also fought regularly for the first time ever with Ben. I turned especially irritable about the way he touched me—but found that after fifteen years, I'd lost the words for what my body wanted. Every time he came and I didn't, which happened about half the times we made love, I felt something different than my usual resigned frustration; I felt murderous rage. I gagged now when I went down on him, choking mad about all the times he didn't go down on me. Even though I was the one smoking, it was my husband's breath that began to smell sour to me.

Shane was the only other smoker in the family, so he and I fell naturally to sneaking around together. Huddled together on his porch overlooking the valley, we lit one another's cigarettes like guilty adolescents. We fanned the smoke away quickly with our hands, cupped the orange embers in our palms.

"I've got to give these up again," I announced once, testing him. I was now buying my cigarettes by the carton, struggling to smoke less than a pack a day.

"I'm not quitting," Shane insisted. "I only smoke four or five an evening, and I enjoy them too much to give them up."

He sat back on his porch swing and gestured for me to join him, but I ignored his invitation, leaning my backside against the wooden railing and eyeing him with envy as he took a deep drag in the half-dark.

"Well, I wish I had your self-control," I said. "If I could smoke that few, I wouldn't want to quit either. But with me, it's all or nothing. I don't know what made me give in to the temptation after all those years."

"Sure you do," Shane said, and I didn't ask him to explain.

When we came in to find Ben and Paula waiting with the drinks and cards, everyone pretended the smell of smoke wasn't clinging to our clothes and hair.

As weeks passed with our two families sharing cookouts and children's parties, I watched Shane in a new way. I watched his hands, their gentleness when he gardened, pushing carefully into the earth. I watched how his dirty blonde hair fell forward over his eyes as he seasoned his perfectly flavored chili. I watched how his long frame folded down to be on eye level with the children as they ran in to show him their clay creations. I watched his smile teasing when he looked at me.

"Hey, beautiful," he always greeted me—and even though he greeted our daughters that way, too, it felt good. Ben rarely used that word.

When the four of us had a few drinks, as we did when we got together to play bridge every Friday night, it got worse. My skin grew so sensitive I could feel every ripple the fabric of my blouse made sliding against my arms and breasts. Eventually, it got so I was damp as soon as I knew we'd be seeing Shane that day. I would sometimes catch myself in a reverie, staring at his mouth. I lost weight without even trying, took more time picking out my clothes for our bridge nights, experimented with new styles for my curly red hair, started applying a little more make-up. I also smoked more every day.

Ben noticed, but thought the sexier look was for him—and that the extra cigarettes were part of some new diet regimen.

"You look great," he told me, smiling, holding me close one night. We'd fought earlier about money, but he gave no indication he remembered. He kissed the side of my neck. His moustache was an irritant I wanted to scratch away.

We were in our bedroom, the warm summer air coming through our window, which overlooked Paula and Shane's house. I was wearing a light summer dress, the barest lingerie underneath. Our girls had already gone to play with Paula and Shane's kids, so we were alone. I could feel Ben's erection pressing into my belly through the dress; it infuriated me.

"You know," I said, shoving him back. "A bit of a warm-up would be nice. I can't just throw my legs open because you've got a hard-on."

He looked stunned. "Honey, I was just giving you a compliment. You always say I don't compliment you enough. I didn't expect us to have sex; Paula and Shane are waiting for us anyway."

Was Shane waiting for me? I wondered. Did he look at himself in the mirror after his showers on the nights when we were going to see one another, his long fingers—those fingers!—running over his flat stomach, water beading on his sunburned back.... I laughed at myself, at the adolescence of this crush.

Guiltily, I turned back to Ben, whose soft, pale skin was as familiar to me as my own. "I'm sorry. I don't know where that came from." And then, as it turned out, we did make love, swiftly, Ben's eyes widening in surprise to find I was moist when his hand grazed against me.

"Touch me," I whispered. "Slow. Slow. Slow." My voice was a mantra, my eyes closed. Ben's fingers tried to go slower, roving over my breasts, down across the rise of my belly and then into the folds of me, but his movements felt awkward, choppy. After a few minutes, we both gave up and reverted to the patterns we knew worked, his hand a blur, hurting me a little, rubbing me fast as he slipped in, bringing me to a hard orgasm, my face on his shoulder.

Afterward, I felt sick; we didn't play bridge that night. I thought if I saw Shane I might cry.

I soon thought of him obsessively. I couldn't tell if he was toying with me in a new way—or if he'd been teasing me for years, naturally flirtatious, and I was only now noticing it. He touched me in as many innocent ways as he could manage, testing my reaction to his hand around my shoulder, or his body touching my back for an instant as he leaned over me to reach for the spices in our kitchen, or his hand steering my hand to the right spot in the night sky as he showed me and the kids the North Star. Each time, I froze completely, afraid any movement or breathing would give me away.

Our passion soon felt to me like the most intense kind, like the white hot center of the embers we buried on our camping trips, the kind that might set the whole forest aflame if one strong breeze blew the top layer off. I daydreamed at work, was distracted with the kids, could barely look at Ben. Our moments on the porch—"our smoking section," Shane called it—were the hardest. Sometimes, when Shane leaned over to light my cigarette, we just stared at one another, our faces inches apart, expressionless and unblinking, our breath suspended in that one moment before I inhaled.

My friendship with Paula was strained—but I couldn't tell if it was my guilt or her sensing what was happening. Our phone calls grew less and less frequent, and when our kids played together, we pretended we had errands to run instead of sitting together watching them and chatting. Ben never said anything; I wondered if he and Paula ever had private sibling talks about us.

Mostly, though, I thought he was just waiting for my unexplained restlessness to blow over. He'd never liked confrontation.

Paula was the one who finally spoke up—focusing all her bitterness on the bad habit we couldn't hide. "This can't go on," she cried out one night, stomping onto the porch after us and dumping an ashtray so furiously that the ashes flew everywhere, coating our clothes and hands. "Ben and I care too much about both of you to watch you destroy yourselves this way. You're not kids, for Gods' sake. You know better."

She yelled so loudly, her youngest woke up and came down crying. "Why is Mommy yelling?" he asked Shane, who hoisted him onto one hip and stared at me over the top of my nephew's blonde head.

"Please," Paula said, her voice low. "If you can't quit for yourselves, at least think of the children."

After that, we took our cigarette breaks separately and furtively, our eyes following one another, our bodies planted firmly beside our spouses'. I tried a nicotine patch, Nicorette gum, a prescription for Welbutrin. I smoked more than ever.

Six months had passed since the bachelorette party. I was daydreaming of divorce. I had never felt so alive.

Shane called me at school one day when he knew Ben was going out of town for the weekend. I was so surprised to hear his voice, I sat down on the edge of a book carrel and sent it toppling, scattering books and startled children everywhere. I struggled to my feet and turned away from the kids to cradle the phone against my ear.

Pretending not to hear the collapse, Shane asked me to help him plan a surprise fortieth birthday party for Paula. After I agreed to meet him for lunch that Saturday, I called Paula and asked her to watch the children. I told her I was having lunch with Janet.

"Happy to do it," she said. "I'll be home all day anyway —Shane's working."

I drove to him in a fog of lust, my mouth open on the freeway, the music almost as loud as my pulse.

Shane was waiting at the bar when I arrived. We smiled when our eyes met, then stood waiting in silence until a hostess showed us to a table.

"Don't tell Ben," Shane said as soon as I sat down. "I want this to be a real surprise, and he has no poker face. He'll give the whole thing away. "

"It will be easier keeping the secret from him than from Paula," I promised. "He's totally oblivious."

We talked like that all through lunch, as if we had nothing else on our minds. Together, we made lists of Paula's friends, planned a menu, chose a date, decided what lies we'd tell so that neither Ben nor Paula would suspect. After two hours, I'd filled the ashtray set between us and gotten drunk on warm rum drinks. When the waitress brought the check, I burst unexpectedly into tears.

"Hey, hey, come on, Carol," Shane said gently. "I think I'd better drive you home."

I blew my nose and turned away from the arm he was offering. He straightened up and nodded.

"OK," he said, as if I'd said something. "I'll take your kids this afternoon so you can nap a little." Then he called Paula on a cell phone from the table and asked her to pack all the children into the van and meet him at the mall for a Disney matinee.

"Yes," I heard him tell her, "the meeting ended early, so I thought it would be fun if we all went out. Just leave Carol a note."

We pretended afterward that nothing had happened—but Shane and I met frequently over the next few weeks, brazenly clandestine, knowing if we were caught we had the perfect excuse. We never touched. We acknowledged nothing. I felt all the time I was with him as if one of my lungs had collapsed, as if I were breathing only half as deeply as I had before I'd started wanting him. I knew better than to blame the cigarettes.

The night of the party was cold and clouded, a grey evening before the sun even set. As we'd arranged, Paula and Ben went together to visit their grandmother in Los Angeles while

Shane and the children and I hung balloons and banners in Paula and Shane's living room. More than forty people were waiting with us—their cars parked a block away—when Paula came home.

The expression on her face was a mixture of delighted shock and something sadder—something that looked like relief. "I knew something was going on," she kept saying, wiping tears from the corners of her eyes. "I knew it. I feel so stupid now."

Ben came in right behind her and stared a moment. "Why didn't you tell me?" he asked accusingly. But Shane and I just laughed, allowing ourselves to believe for a moment that everything was as innocent as it appeared.

I was doing the dishes hours later, standing at their sink, when Shane came up behind me to reach for a glass from the cabinet over my head. I tried to keep rinsing the bowl in my hand, swirling the steaming, soapy water around and around, not breathing. But this time, the contact between our bodies kept on—he stayed there, breathing slowly and deeply, his arm stretched over my head reaching into the cabinet, his body just barely against me. I could feel every inch of him, the heat of him surrounding me like the steam and spray from the sink. I realized I'd been holding my breath only when it came out with a shuddering little sound.

I let my hands sink into the water, releasing the bowl. My head fell forward, showing him the back of my neck, and I felt him sigh with pleasure at my reaction. And then I could feel him growing hard against my back, alive under the loose pants he was wearing. His arousal worked powerfully on me. Knowing he was hard for me, I felt my legs turn liquid.

I didn't dare say a word. I was incredibly aroused, trembling, but afraid any sound or movement on my part would encourage him—or scare him away. I didn't know which I wanted to happen—or I did, but was afraid to play any active role.

He spoke first, after what seemed endless time: "For the last few months," he said—and those first words brought a choked sob up in my throat. His voice was so low I wouldn't have recognized it if I couldn't smell him behind me. "I've tried everything," he started again, "but I can't stop thinking about you. I'm living in daydreams. Carol, I know you. I've watched you. You daydream, too. Tell me your fantasies about me."

I made a strange, hoarse, laughing sound, my hands still under the running water, my head still facing the darkened window in front of the sink. We hadn't looked at one another yet.

"I'm living one right now," I finally said. "You know that."

He leaned closer, drawing in a deep breath, rubbing his cheek very gently against my hair. "Details," he insisted. "What do you think about?"

I wanted to tell him. I'd always loved talking about sex, sharing fantasies. Ben wouldn't—couldn't—grew uncomfortable when I did. Shane was the only man I knew who seemed to enjoy talking about sex as much as most women I knew.

"Tell me," he said, his breath a warm whisper moving my hair. "Tell me—just one fantasy."

An image forced its way in: him kneeling before me, his fingertips lightly resting on my thighs, his nose less than an inch from my darker red, curling hair, his face rapturous as he breathed me in, my legs quivering under his touch, my body falling open as I slid to the floor. I saw hour after hour of his teasing, hours in which he never grew impatient or tired or bored, hours in which I believed for the first time my body deserved such attention.

I lifted my head and caught him staring at my reflection in the window. "No," I said, sharply.

He immediately moved away and leaned back against the counter, waiting for me to come to him. Now that we faced one another, a first kiss was a palpable possibility. I felt nearly faint with guilt and desire. It was this kiss, the first moment our lips would come together—or even the moment before, when our faces were closing in—that had possessed most of my thoughts. But neither of us moved, our eyes locked, our wanting so intense it felt as if we were already seared together.

"We don't have to do anything," he said finally. "I've never been unfaithful to Paula. We can just talk. You can tell me your daydreams, I can tell you mine, and we can go home to our own beds more turned on because of it."

The thought of him bringing this energy—sexual energy I had fueled—home to Paula made me burn with rage and longing. I would combust if just one of his fingers touched me.

"I can't," I managed. "Leave now."

And then, as if I'd willed him to appear, Ben walked into the kitchen. I turned back to the sink, returned to the dishes, heard Shane walk out. When my husband came up behind me and kissed the nape of my neck, I'm sure the ferocity of my passion took him by surprise. I whirled around and brought my wet soapy hands up to grip his face and kiss him fiercely, moaning against him, my body grinding with need. We had fast, furious sex right against the sink, with me doing little more than lifting my peasant skirt to impale myself on him. I held the sink with one slippery hand and used the other to rub myself, my fingers swirling as my husband filled me. Ben still talks about that night as one of our best.

"Fifteen years of marriage, and you are still so wild," he said afterward, kissing the tip of my nose. "Where do you get the energy?"

We were sitting on the kitchen floor, not caring who might come in—or maybe caring but sitting there defiantly anyway, our legs sprawled, leaving our mark on one another and on Shane's kitchen. When I rolled over to stand up, we both heard the crinkle of cellophane as the cigarettes in my hip pocket ground against the floor.

"Careful," Ben said lazily. "You'll crush the whole pack."

"It doesn't matter," I told him. "I'm quitting now."

Iris Litt

The Stuff

Phil just wanted to be left alone. By mosquitos and people. I like to keep the patio doors open, but I have to keep them closed because the mosquitos go straight for him. I read in the New York Times that mosquitos are attracted by ill temper. You'd think they'd run away from it, but they apparently find interpersonal friction exciting, the way some people go for adversarial people. Am I an insect because I went for Phil?

We were staying in San Lucas, a beautifully-preserved Colonial mountain town, and I was getting interested in Mexican medicine. I mean, they don't exactly have a national health system, so being on their own that way, they have become amazingly inventive.

At any rate, during the *comida corrida* at a local hangout, I complained to Maria and Carmen and George and the rest of the gringo gang about how stuffy our room was due to Phil's mosquito problem, which led to the further problem of our needing the ceiling fan whose wind was agonizingly strong because its lowest setting is stuck at Number Five.

"We've asked the owner many times if he can 'arreglar' it, but he says that's impo-siblay."

"So you have a choice between fresh air with mosquitos or suffocation or wind torture," said Maria sympathetically. Then, as one who prided herself on having wellness information available at all times, she added thoughtfully, "There's an old woman who lives way up the hill above the mercado who sells stuff that keeps mosquitos and other critters away."

Maria believed this substance might also keep scorpions and snakes away, and I wondered aloud if it contained the same ingredients that keep deer away up north; I think it's made from some substance of the yew tree or some other piney stuff.

After comida, I kept thinking about it. I lay down next to Phil for siesta. He reached out his big arms and snuggled me against him. "Come wriggle up to this snarling, snorting rhino," he said. At least Phil was honest in his self-descriptions. These were the moments I loved with Phil, when he pulled me close against his hairy chest and baby-smooth beer belly and fell off contentedly to sleep. I had grown very fond of his beer belly. When we lay in the spoon position, with me cuddled up against his back, I draped my arm over him and rested my hand on his belly. It was surprisingly firm, and it gave me the feeling that I had something to hold on to. It made lying under the overkill of the ceiling fan okay. It even made Phil's frequent ill temper and annoying habits seem worth it.

Anyhow, before I fell asleep, I thought about the woman above the mercado and her potion. If it worked and Phil stopped being so scared of mosquitos, we could leave the patio doors open and the ceiling fan off. Up north, whenever I thought of Mexico. I thought of the air—the walls that let the breezes through, the open doors, the glassless windows. I thought of being in a room with all doors and windows open and, outside, churchbells bonging, parrots screeching, children shouting, donkeys braying. Yet here I was now, in Mexico, cooped up in a room with the doors closed under a ceiling fan that was really a tornado.

I decided that it would be well worth the orthopedically devastating climb up the hill from the mercado to investigate the magical mosquito deterrent. Even if the stuff wasn't available, perhaps I'd learn more about the other magical Mexican medicines the lady guru stocked. And even if it was available and didn't work, it would probably cost only a few pesos which, thanks to a recent devaluation, would translate into an American dollar or less.

The old lady turned out not to be so old; she just looked old to gringos. In fact, she may not have been older than me. She had the wrinkled face but dark hair without a trace of gray so common in local women. She smiled the bright, guileless smile of the San Lucas people.

I described the substance I wanted in my less-than-perfect Spanish, and she seemed to know immediately what I meant.

"He doesn't like mosquitos, eh," she said. She smiled, revealing a total of four teeth.

"No, but they like him."

She laughed. "Is he *nervioso*?"

"Well, yes."

"Mosquitos like that."

I was tempted to tell her that distinguished scientists had recently agreed with her in the pages of the Estados Unidos' most prestigious newspaper, but I decided not to complicate the conversation. Besides, she had taken a large bottle off the shelf and was pouring some into a small bottle which she held out to me.

"This is Esencia de Arbol." A rather non-committal name, I thought: Essence of Tree.

"Tell him to use plenty. It will keep everything away. *Todos*."

"How about people?" I asked, thinking it a joke.

"*Puede ser*," she said. Could be.

"I think my friend might like that."

I gave her the five pesos and left.

Making my way down the steep cobblestone streets, I thought about how Phil was when it came to people.

"I'm not interested in spending time with strangers," he'd say.

"They're not strangers," I'd say. "We've seen them three times and you said you liked them."

"They're strangers," he'd insist.

So when I ran into Betty and George Barrett coming out of the mercado and they said they were having some people over on the sixteenth, I knew that getting him to this social event, like any other, would require artistry. This time I told him about an engineering professor from the States who would be there, and he finally agreed to consider attending:

"All right, but I'm just going to sit in a corner. Don't, I repeat, do not, introduce me to anyone."

"I promise," I said resignedly. I went out to the patio and sat there, remembering miserably the last time I had violated this vow. We are going to Rio Grande to get Phil's tooth fixed. I run into Janet, an engaging young lady whom we met at Carmen's party. Thinking of our badly-dented budget, I ask Janet if she wants to share a cab from the bus station in Rio Grande to the dentist's neighborhood. She beams and says Yes. I am feeling happy; I am among friends. I put my arm around Phil's waist and beam back at her.

On the bus, he turns to me suddenly and says:

"Do you have to invite strangers to go with us?"

I am overcome by shock and a kind of innocent amazement. "She's not a stranger. We've already exchanged cards. We talked about keeping in touch. You said you liked her."

"That doesn't matter. You make a fool of yourself, always talking to strangers. They're laughing at you."

"Clearly a statement by a paranoid person. And how about all the things you do? I don't say a thing when you do your control-freak thing with the guy at the hotel desk."

"Just don't include me in your friendly overtures."

"I don't include you."

"*They* think I'm included."

I turn away. I feel that my heart is broken because he sees me in such a dark way. Because he is so suspicious, so distrustful of me. Because this thing I have, this quality that my friends value in me—a kind of ability to make warm contact—is so abhorrent to him. Because he is so different from me. And because I feel I should leave him.

When I think of leaving him, the tears dribble pitifully down my cheeks from under my dark glasses.

If I stay with him, I will be locked into a little invisible cage, a caged bird; bad enough to be caged but worse to be forbidden to reach out when a friendly face appears beyond the bars.

It was almost as though I had known there would be such a scene today, because I had brought with me a giant size box of kleenex in my favorite soft, flowered travel container.

I suggested to Phil that we give Esencia de Arbol a try.

We stood in the middle of the room and I applied the oily liquid to his pulse points. He was docile and appreciative. At these times he was incredibly lovable.

I stroked the stuff on his wrists, behind his ears, and at his throat and on his ankles. Then we turned off the fan, threw open the patio doors, fell onto the bed and made love. Afterward, we lay there as the sky grew pink with sunset and the churchbells bonged. No mosquitos appeared.

I am a happy woman, I thought. He put his big arms around me for a frontal snuggle. But something was wrong. There was a faint odor about him, something different and I, who never tire of snuggling, stayed at a slight distance, attracted as always by his presence but indefinably repelled.

Of course. The Stuff. Now I could leave the patio doors open and the ceiling fan off, but now I would have to live with this vaguely repellent odor. Of course, that's what it was—a repellent. But I hadn't expected it to repel *me*.

An hour before Betty and George's party, Phil asked, "Why am I going to this party?"

It was a tape we played so frequently—at least once before every social event—that I unthinkingly recited my party line, you should pardon the pun, while concentrating on splashing on a quick coat of "Tropic Coral" nail polish to hide the peeled-off places.

"We're going to this party," I recited, "because we said we would."

"Why did I say I would?"

"Because deep down you wanted to go."

"The hell I did. I said I'd go because I knew you wanted me to. I did it for you."

"Thank you. I appreciate that."

"All right, I'm going to go, but not for more than an hour and a half, and I may decide to sit in a corner and not talk to anyone."

"Fine with me."

The cocktail parties on San Lucas terraces, patios and rooftops began while the sun was still bright on the mountains, then became sunset-watching parties as the sky grew lavender and the brilliant pink of the bougainvillea splashed against the lavender as it faded to navy blue. As the colors grew cooler, the air grew cooler, too, and as the guests' degree of inebriation increased, so did the spirit of warmth and fun.

Of course, this made Phil's corner-sitting behavior all the more incongruous but his old acquaintances had gotten used to it. Usually I would see someone approach him with innocent friendliness and then back away when his insularity became apparent. But tonight no one seemed to notice him and no one approached him.

From the corner of the rooftop diagonally opposite Phil, I saw him gesturing to Carlos, the street dog whom Betty and George had befriended. Carlos had never forgotten his cruel and lean first year of sleeping in potholes and begging for food with his huge eyes. Now he was plump as few Mexican dogs are.

A taxi driver had said to me reassuringly when he had narrowly missed hitting a dog: "La vida de un perro no vale nada." The life of a dog is worth nothing. So I think Carlos knew that he had found an incomparably good thing in the love of these gringos. His personality seemed to me to be similar to my own: he was determined to enjoy every minute of his life.

When Phil held up a ham hors d'oeuvre and clucked affectionately, Carlos approached and stopped about two feet away, visibly salivating. Then his head sagged, his eyes closed, and he turned and walked away.

On the way home, we walked through the town *jardin*. In the central gazebo, mariachis played. Lovers strolled. Families frolicked. The moon hovered as in a postcard behind the cathedral spires.

I reached for Phil's hand.

"It was fine, wasn't it?" I asked rhetorically. "No one bothered you. Not even Carlos."

"It was okay," he said crossly.

I pushed aside the insidious little chill I experienced when I could tell that Phil was in one of his negative moods. You can't blame me, can you? Phil's bad mood meant that it would be hard for me to enjoy anything until he got into a better one. I tried to stay unperturbed.

"Let's sit down on a bench," I suggested. "It's such a perfect night."

"Not me," he said. "You stay if you want."

I knew that at home I'd be punished by absolute silence, a bizarre, undiluted, unalleviated stillness in which any of my attempts at conversation would lie there like a *latke*.

When I got really tired of his moods, I generally let him go on home alone, and that's what I did tonight. Somehow, I didn't seem to be feeling the usual disappointment and anger I felt when his ill-temper interrupted what could have been a delicious night. Here we were in the *jardin*, Mexico's version of the Garden of Eden, with the balmy breeze blowing and the moon riding high, and he was going home. No problem for me to enjoy it alone. After he had left, it was obvious that I didn't have to be alone if I didn't want to. Several gringos came along and said Hi, and an incredibly handsome man sat down near me and started a conversation. He was from Mexico City, urbane and knowledgeable, and his voice was deep and soft and naturally seductive. But I knew that I was not the least bit available. Despite my problems living with Phil, it was as though some Crazy Glue had set between us.

I told my new acquaintance that my husband was waiting for me and picked my way back home over the familiar cobblestone streets. Phil was sitting in the armchair watching CNN and reading one of his engineering books. Whereas I like silence in the room and listening to the sounds outside, Phil always turns on the TV or radio as soon as he enters a room, as though filling the vacuum created by his own self-imposed silences. In line with his usual maintenance of the status quo, he had not opened the patio doors, which he insists we close, for security reasons, whenever we go out, even though crime is rare in San Lucas.

I went to the patio doors and pulled out the black wrought-iron bolts. Outside, I sat and inhaled the view: the dark ridge of mountains, the turrets of several churches, the bougainvillea scrambling over the tile rooftops.

Then I heard Phil's voice, more strident than usual.

"Do you realize that no one said a fucking word to me during that whole fucking party?"

I turned sideways in my chair and faced him through the open double door.

"You said that was what you wanted."

"Well, maybe, to a point."

"You mean that you want to be able to lay down the law, your don't-speak-to-me law, but you want them all to be available in case you change your mind."

"Thank you for that five-cent byte of pop psychology."

When we got into bed, he turned his back to me and moved a few inches away. I lay on my side in a potential spoon position with this huge two-inch gulf between us, looking out the open patio door at the moon above the mountains and rooftops. Once again, I didn't mind this distance as much as I used to. In a way I was happy to stay at a distance from that faint piney odor, as though the forest had turned sour. No mosquitos approached, nor did I.

We had breakfast in one of the courtyard restaurants that made life in San Lucas so pleasant. Betty and George came in with Carlos trotting beside them, and then Maria and Carmen and Janet came in and joined them. They all waved, and I called out how great the party had been, and everyone smiled but no one attempted to join us nor did Carlos come forward to access his hoped-for snack. He settled under their table as they talked and laughed, and stared out at us with what I believed was reproach.

We finished our breakfast in silence and Phil said abruptly, "Will you take care of the check? I can't stand dealing with that imbecile," glaring at the smiling waiter.

He walked ahead of me on the sidewalk that was wide enough for only one person, and threw remarks at me over his shoulder.

"What the hell is the matter with them all? I never saw so many unfriendly sleazy types."

"Phil," I said firmly, "turn here and we're going to sit in the *jardin*."

We sat on a bench facing the cathedral. I paid the six-year-old newsboy for the Mexico City News. Bright balloons floated ahead of us, street vendors hawked, and at the stalls on the plaza, brilliantly colored fabrics and baskets and paintings and tiles formed a kaleidoscope. Huge white clouds blew past on a fresh wind. The time had come, I decided, to move on to a new era.

"Phil," I said gently, "you must stop putting that stuff on."

"You think the stuff is doing it?"

"I know it."

"How do you know?"

"I just know."

"I'll think it over," he said. In case I've neglected to mention it, Phil never agrees to anything immediately.

We went back to the room, which was warm and airless compared with the mountain breeziness outside, and I checked my natural impulse to go straight to the patio doors and open them.

"Take a shower," I said. "And you can put the fan on."

I often reflected how strange it was that when I *really* meant something, he did it.

He set the fan on its low of five, and disappeared into the shower. I gave pious thanks when I heard the water running, since it didn't run every day.

I got under the covers so the tornado above wouldn't chill me. He came out and lay down beside me and put his forearm over his eyes as though in torment, or at the very least, indecision.

"So you think that stuff is really potent," he said.

"Well, it might help reduce the birthrate of Mexico," I said brightly, "which would be good since they figure there will be fifty million people in he Valley of Mexico by the year whatever."

He didn't respond, so I added, "We could go back to the way we were before."

"It wasn't so bad, was it?"

"It was pretty bad."

"But it's bearable, isn't it, my little cichlid?" A cichlid is a kind of fish that is noted for rubbing its body against its mate's. It had become Phil's term of advanced endearment, and he used it when he was feeling extraordinarily affectionate toward me.

He reached out and pulled me against him, every inch of us head to toe touching, his beer belly in the space between my breasts and my belly, our knees and toes handsomely coordinated. Above our heads, I heard the buzz of a mosquito.

"Eminently bearable," I said.

Peter Cooper

Opal Moon

Spare light struggled through the gauze curtain and Juan Miguel turned his head toward the window, meeting it halfway. How funny that this pale gold should arrive after the brilliant silver of the previous night's full moon. Like this weak sun, he barely had the energy for this last day. But like the sun, he too must rise, cross the surly hours that lay ahead. He knew he would make it to the evening, but he had little ambition.

He pushed apart the curtains, looked up at the flat, cloudless blue split by a pair black electric lines that linked his small shop and apartment to the rest of the town. Last night, the nearly full moon had rested for the longest while there, a canny tightrope walker pondering his next trick. And just like the circus, that old moon had sat there, building up the anticipation of its singular audience, before catapulting away, skimming the top of that black canvas of night.

Juan Miguel, tired after a full day of the close-out sale, had closed the curtain and gone to bed. Like waking and sleeping, every journey started in the east ends in the west.

Rising, he pulled the nightshirt over his head and walked to the toilet. He leaned over the small basin and splashed water on his face, smiling at his enduring wonder over the miracle of hot and cold running water. There had been a time when a cold mountain stream was his only source of drink and cleanliness. Scrubbing his manicured fingers, he appreciated the smoothness of his skin, sure signs of his hard won gentility. These same hands had once been tough as claws, scratching and invading the dark walls of the mines in the wilds of Chile—another place of beginning and ending.

Dressing carefully, he glanced at the small assortment of rings on his dresser, decided against them. True, a jeweler should be an example to his customers—an inspiration—but this was his last day in business. He would leave as humbly as he arrived.

Besides, there was only one ring left to sell, and he had even toyed with the idea of keeping it as the final memento of the shop. There had been so many people yesterday, descending like piranhas on the flesh of his going-out-of-business. He had been struck by the fact that only this one clear opal on a silver band remained when he closed at five. Mildly superstitious, he had struggled to find the meaning of this lone orphaned gem. Was he to take it to the ocean and toss it in, a repayment to the gods for giving him the small bliss of wealth that would see him to the end of his life? Or was he to keep it as a reminder of his days as a merchant?

Watching the moon the night before, he thought he understood. Closing the shop, he had noticed the opal, hidden in a fold of black velvet on the empty display. One bright reminder of the lifetime of diamonds that had once sprinkled the shelf like stars, each now carried away by a thirty-year continuum of lovers. For three decades they arrived, hands knotted in terrified anticipation, hopefully grazing the silver and gold bands adorned by celestial slivers which Juan Miguel had so lovingly set in place. He had understood his role, a priest of the earth bestowing this mineral blessing on their desire to be together forever, linked by precious strands and gleaming chunks of night sky.

Living in this town for so long, he had watched them engage, marry, gather children around them, and grow old. As they passed his window, he was saddened by the fact that they never again held hands as when they selected their rings. Though once, when he had gone to the small hospital to have stitches put in a cut, he had seen two of his customers. The man lay on a gurney, dying from a heart attack. Too young, both he and his wife carried that same terror in their faces as when they first entered his shop.

They clutched each other's hands, the confusion of this awful ending so similar to their hopeful beginning.

He had hurried out, taped up his ankle. It healed on its own.

But he could not fault them. He too had been such a fool as to believe in the eternal possibilities of love. Shaking his head, he walked down the narrow steps to the silent shop. Hard to believe that he had once been a boisterous youth, tanned and vigorous in the Guadalajara sun. Back then, he had existed on the other side of jewelry. A ring meant romantic possession, not commerce. He and his friends would sit on the long wall that led to the plaza, watching the pretty girls becoming women, dreaming of putting a ring on one of their fingers. They had become experts at seeing left hands from a hundred yards, searching out the glint that said they were already taken, or the absence of sparkle, which meant...so many things to a young, hungry heart.

Carefully pouring the coffee grounds in the water pot, Juan Miguel reached to turn on the burner. He had never lost his taste for camp coffee, finding filtered brew too weak and sophisticated for his taste. Another reminder of his years in Chile where the miners slept out under the stars, then threw the coffee into the boiling pot of water. It was a hard taste, but their life had been hard. Wrestling with Mother Earth to steal a few minor treasures took courage and numbing perseverance. Her guardians were the hot sun and frozen winds, and digging a new shaft was not unlike making love to a dangerous virgin. There was no way of telling when she would crush you by closing her legs, or take a hand, arm or leg in payment for her favors.

He skimmed out the grounds and sat down with his cup, reaching for a cigarette. That had not been his first ambition. As a town boy, he was schooled well enough in numbers and words to become a clerk. Indeed, his mother and father had been so proud when he landed that first job at seventeen, cleaning and stacking the shelves at the small pharmacy. The "Doctor" was so impressive in his white lab coat, mixing the magical powders in such exact proportions.

Now, Juan Miguel understood that the man was just another kind of clerk, trading his packets for pesos. But to a boy with little money and shallow prospects, the Doctor was a mystical shaman. Whenever the medicine worked, the patients would come and bless him for his assistance and knowledge. When the medicine failed, they would all shake their heads.

"Even the Doctor cannot save those whom God has decided to call home."

Juan Miguel too had believed in the power of the man, the wisdom of God. He had been no different. He would watch, leaning on his broom, as the customers came and confessed their ailments, looking up hopefully at the Doctor, waiting for his dispensation.

But a real priest did not have children, and while the Doctor was a widower, he did have a daughter. Her name was Luna, and she was bright as her name, nearly as mysterious. Juan Miguel would watch star-struck whenever she entered the store to deliver her father's lunch. Sitting on the long wall that led to the plaza, he was never embarrassed about his simple clothing, his ordinary looks. But when she came to the pharmacy, he would blush with shame at his very existence. And she teased him.

"Your face is sunburned, Juan," she told him. "You must be careful when you go outside."

And the red would increase.

"Have you burned your tongue? You never speak when I am here."

He would turn away miserably, shaken by the way love could cut so easily.

For a year she teased him. Outside the shop, he listened for news of her everywhere, finding ways to introduce her name into conversation, hoping someone else would know of her intentions in life. But all he heard were tales of her laughter at parties and sly hints about unchaperoned dates.

One afternoon he was cleaning the back room when he heard two women idly chatting by the counter while they waited for the Doctor to fill their prescriptions.

"He is such a good father," the older one sighed. "It is a shame that he had to have such a bad daughter."

Juan Miguel moved to the edge of the back door.

The other woman crossed herself. "Imagine, to become pregnant and not know who the father is? The Doctor must be terribly ashamed."

"They say he still doesn't know. How could he, with no wife to watch her?"

"Still, someone will have to step forward. She surely won't have the child without some kind of husband."

"But who would marry her? What man wants that kind of girl?"

The Doctor stepped from behind his glass cage and the two ended their conversation abruptly. Juan Miguel leaned against the doorjamb. As stunned as he was by the malicious information, he also realized that God had given him an opportunity. If no self-respecting man would marry her, maybe she could consider marrying a lowly clerk like him.

That next morning, he took his savings from a small box in the bottom of the dresser. One hundred and fifty-six pesos, three pesos a week for the whole year he had worked. He rolled the bills into a ball and tied it with string. He felt funny walking to work, the lump in his pocket seemed too conspicuous, and everyone he passed seemed to notice. Brushing aside their imagined glances, he slipped into the pharmacy, on time as usual.

"Doctor," he said. "May I have a few minutes this morning to run an errand for my mother?"

"Of course, Juan Miguel," the doctor said from behind his glass cage. "But be quick. I'm expecting many customers today."

Juan Miguel hurried up the street to the jewelry store. The old man behind the display cases squinted at him.

"Can I help you, boy?"

"I need a ring."

"Ah, a token of friendship for a girlfriend?"

Juan Miguel shook his head. "An engagement ring."

The squint rounded, the old man brushed his hands. "You are very young, boy, for such an important step. You should wait until you can at least grow a mustache."

If there were another jeweler in the town, Juan Miguel would have left immediately. "The mustache can wait. I need a ring today, this morning."

Sighing, the old man pulled out a tray. "Here are some very nice rings, and not very expensive."

"I have one hundred and seventy-five pesos. I'm not worried about cost."

Chuckling, the man replaced the tray with another. "These are better, they come from Chile, stones that are very hard to find."

"I want a diamond. She must wear a diamond."

"Diamonds are good, it's true," the old man said. "But they can be too bright. Sometimes they blind the person who wears them. All stones come from the earth, each with their own song. Do you want her to see you or the ring?"

Juan Miguel blushed. How did this codger know so much? "Please, I have to hurry back to work."

"So fast." the old man clucked his tongue. "If I were your age again, I would go to Chile, work the mines, and find the perfect stone, one that expressed exactly who I was. It would take months, maybe years. And when I found just that stone, then I would come back and find the right woman—one who wanted exactly that stone, because it reminded her of me."

Gritting his teeth, Juan Miguel pointed through the case to a small gold ring with a single diamond. "How much is that one?"

"One eighty-five."

Miguel shook his head. "How about that one?"

The old man put his hand on the counter. "Wouldn't you rather look at the first tray? If that is all your money, how will you live? Getting married costs more than the price of the ring."

"I know that, but I have no time. Please, I have to get back to work. Show me a diamond I can afford."

Reaching into the display, the old man took out a small diamond cluster. "This is the only one I have, I'm afraid."

"Then that's the one I want."

Miguel gave him the money, then took the small box and hurried back to the pharmacy. He cleaned furiously, looking constantly at the clock. At twelve-thirty, Luna entered, swinging her father's lunch nonchalantly. The Doctor took the box and walked out back to the small table behind the store. As she headed for the front door, Juan Miguel stepped forward to intercept her.

"Luna?"

She turned, flashed a bright smile. "Ah, I see your tongue has healed. You can speak."

Juan Miguel fought his embarrassment, slipped his hand into his pocket to hold the ring box for courage.

"Yes, I can. May I speak with you for a moment?"

"So formal?" She placed her hand on her hip, tilting her head back. "Yes, you may speak."

"I-I know you're in trouble."

Her eyes darkened. "What trouble?"

"I know. I just know." God, give me courage. "I would like to help you. I would be honored to help you."

"What help..."

He pulled out the small box, pushed it toward her.

She took it, opened it slowly and frowned.

"But this is a ring." She closed the box. "Why do I need a ring?"

"I would be happy to marry you."

Her eyes widened.

"They are all saying that no one would marry you, but they are wrong. I would marry you today, this very minute. I would like to help you prove them wrong."

A glint of laughter invaded her eyes, but she pushed it away.

"What makes you think I want to get married?"

"For the baby, of course." He blushed. "I do not care if you don't know who the father is, I would be a very good father."

"What makes you think there is a baby?"

"They say—"

"They are wrong! They talk and talk and talk, and you listen and listen. You are a fool, Juan Miguel with the burned tongue." She threw the box at him. "I liked you better when you didn't talk, at least then I didn't know how stupid you are."

He caught the box, jammed it into his pocket.

"You tell all those crows who have nothing to do but squawk that they can talk about someone else, because I am not who they think I am." She jammed her finger into his chest. "And I am not who you think I am either."

Ashamed, Juan Miguel watched her go. Fool! Fool! He ground his fists into his temple. How could he be so stupid?

That day, he barely finished his cleaning. As he walked down the street, two women pointed at him and laughed. Then several children seemed to be making a joke of him as well.

He was able to get to the jeweler just as the old man was closing his doors.

"Please, Old Man, I need to—"

With sad eyes, the man nodded, motioned Juan Miguel inside. He took the ring and handed him the ball of pesos, still tied.

"I'm sorry it didn't work out for you, but I knew." He shook his head. "I hate knowing."

The next morning, Juan Miguel packed his clothes into a canvas bag and made his way to the train station. He never went back to Guadalajara.

Pulling open the shutters, Juan Miguel's hand trembled. It was indeed silly to open for just one gem, but what better did he have to do with this day? As he gazed up the empty street, he suddenly noticed a young farmer heading toward the shop. Juan Miguel quickly went back behind the counter, watched as the young man peered in through the window, then opened the door.

"Do you have nothing left?"

Juan Miguel shrugged. "Just one ring."

"Can I see it?"

They both looked down at the shimmering opal, so much like the moon on the black velvet sky. The young man reached into his pocket.

"Is this enough? I must have it today."

Juan Miguel chuckled. "If I were your age, I would take myself to Chile and work the mines. Find the stone that represented exactly who I was—then I would come back and look for a woman. Not the other way around."

The young man looked up. "That is good advice, I will remember it when I begin to look for a wife."

Flustered, Juan Miguel looked at his last customer. Then he saw it, a terrible sadness in the young eyes.

"I am sorry, my friend. I thought you..."

He nodded, though there was water in his eyes. "It is for my grandmother. She raised me after my parents died. She had a hard life, never married herself. But she was very proud, even right to the end." His voice cracked. "She never wore jewelry, but I thought if I could slip a ring on her finger before she went to God, then maybe he would bless her. She was a very good woman."

He offered the money. It was moist and dirty, but honestly earned. Juan Miguel folded it back into the man's hand.

"This is my gift to you and your good grandmother."

Astonished, the young man put the ring in one pocket, the money back into the other. He cast about for a moment, needing to tell this kind merchant something more for his generosity.

"She refused to go to the hospital. She said it was a waste of money." His voice cracked. "She told me 'Even the Doctor cannot save those whom God has decided to call home.' And now, God has called her."

He turned and started toward the door. Then stopped. "May I know your name, sir. I would like to tell her of your kindness.

Juan Miguel shook his head, smiling sadly. "She is in heaven, so she already knows it."

Alone again, Juan Miguel sat for a few minutes, then rose to close the shutters and lock the door. He smiled as he glanced out at the street, noticing the tall church steeple at the end of the block. He was pretty sure the woman was not his Luna, but he thanked God for showing him that he had not been such a stupid boy after all.

Inside his chest, he could feel the moon rising, growing fuller and fuller. It smiled with him.

Nicole Quinn

The Man with the Watch

The man with the watch is curled up on his side. A small smile sets the corners of his mouth. His lips are blue-tinged, azure married to silver grey. The color of sky at the dawn of a brilliant day. His eyelids are open, just a crack. The dull sheen of iris in lantern light an eerie effect. Almost a twinkle. His clothes are coal-smudged dungarees, hung loosely on a spare frame. He seems quite comfortable cozied there. Just taking an afternoon snooze amidst the rubble of the collapsed mine.

German. That's what they're speaking. The others. All four talking at once, in a frenzy to have the story told the right way. The rescuers, surprised that they're able to speak at all. Let alone breathe.

Six days. Five men. By all calculations there shouldn't have been enough air to last half that long.

"How have you managed it? To survive."

The four cast their eyes toward the man with the watch. They hang their heads. In reverence. In shame. In gratitude.

It had been almost quitting time when the world gave in. Frantic shouts. Lone voices swallowed in the din of destruction. Chaos was cacophonous, followed by the numbing quiet, randomly punctuated by the straggler rock rushing to catch up to the others as a shroud of dust settled on the fresh grave.

Helmet lanterns flashed beams in frantic darts across the granite ceiling. Voices were raised in hopeful queries. Names pronounced. A role call for the dead, fleeting elation for the living.

One of them. Armin. Or Ulrich. One of them had heaved himself against the two ton escarpment now separating them from the tunnel, still a half mile from the sky. Hands. Makeshift shovels of bone, tattered skin, and blood, no match for the geology grown used to dynamite and pick axes, useless against the immovable mass.

Once the tears had become gentle moans and muffled murmurs, survival talk began. The air hose, how much oxygen? Three days. Maybe four. Weighing the odds of rescue on a life and death scale. The balance shifting toward extinction. The hours formally tolled by the man with the watch.

Hunger came next. Followed by thirst. The remains of lunch buckets examined and rationed. Repasts lovingly packed by Olaf's wife and Ulrich's girlfriend. The red-haired one whose yards of thigh all of them had noticed and admired. Crusts of sandwichs. Mutton and ham. Sips of tea. Hansy's mother's idea of supper was a loaf of bread and block of cheese the size of her son's big round head. A bar meal of sausages and boiled eggs had been purchased from old Otto who kept the tavern near Armin's small let room. Food he would never eat. His stomach a turbulent sea of last night's whiskey and cigarettes, heaped upon the same of innumerable nights before. He even had a jug of cheap beer, to indulge his habit turned need. The withdrawal from which would haunt at least two of their nights. Or were they days? No one would know. But the man with the watch.

The stench of the chamber was impossible to ignore. What little air was left to them polluted as feces rotted to methane and rodents scurried there in the dark. Quarrels broke out. Some came to blows. Ulrich's hidden chocolate bar and Armin's secret flask. Hans snored and Olaf's knuckles needed to knock flesh on a regular basis. Snouted nostrils flaring there in the gloom. Horned creatures who resembled the miners in every way but fear. Each beast determined to survive.

Greta would worry, thought the man with the watch. She would have been waiting on the slope of the hill, counting the minutes till he would round the bend. Hungry for him. Letting him take her there on the coarse grass where she grazed her goats. Her hair, the color and scent of hay reaped and piled in random mounds. Breaths heaved upon the earth. Eager to re-consummate their two month old union. Time suspended, for the moment.

She'd given him the watch as a wedding present, knowing that he wouldn't always be in the mine. Just until they could afford to move on. A big city maybe. An office somewhere. Yes, Greta would worry. He was always on time.

Time took on new meaning, there in the dark. A soft phosphorous glow off a face with three hands. He'd stared at the watch interminably, the only friend he now knew. No one bothered him, huddled against the cool stone of the far wall, giddy with power. The days shaped at his whim. He'd made the revolution of the earth twice, and sometimes three times as long as Julius had. Minding the minutes. Conning the hours. Watching his compatriots unknowingly defy logic. He had taken on the mantle of the almighty, creating, there in the shadows, twice as many days. Twice as much time.

The air had gotten thin. It worried the man with the watch. The pain in his chest crushing his lungs into the stone. He'd scrutinized the others for some sign of decline. Startled by the ruddy cheeks and robust voices. The erratic antics that only full lungs could achieve. They'd believed in the world he had shaped. An hour knelled after some three had passed. Only he held the truth of the watch, trapped in the limited reality of its works. Only he knew they ought to be dying.

Greta. His Greta. Water dripped from his eyes. He had imagined her old. The map of their lives together etched across sagging skin. A landscape of wrinkles key coded by children all grown. Greta. Her scent filled the weak flow of air. Lambs and lavender. Clover fields wet with summer rain. Greta. Alone in a world where clocks kept the pace, tick-ticking away.

Rage welled in the man who kept time. His breath wheezed on a thin wail of lament for the life left unlived. The airless portion of his brain summoned evil thoughts. Wicked deeds. It would have been easy to accelerate the hours. Die in a crowd. The timepiece turned weapon spewing its poison on the unsuspecting. No one need know that he had played god.

His eyes rested on the others. Innocents cased in world-weary hulls. He'd chuckled, a raspy choking sound, noting the worried glances cast his way, faces sculpted by fear. His grip on the watch tightened. He felt the cool of the metal, the smooth leather of its band. His thumb caressed the thick crystal, clearly masking the truth. He'd smiled, knowing full well the knowledge would be buried with him, when he ran out of time.

Olaf remembers him beginning to fade. Clutching that watch in the death grip of his skeletal hand. Calling out the hours even as the last breath parted his lips. His chest had rattled. Gasping, as if for air, though they'd all known, they'd had at least two days to spare.

Ulrich recalls how he had rallied near the end. Summoning some reserve strength to dash the timepiece on an outcrop of shale. Bits of broken glass. Sprockets and springs. The act pleasing him somehow.

Hansy shudders as he says goodbye. Armin's eyes are wet.

"We spoke to him of the daylight. The moon. The stars."

All the whiles of the universe certain to anchor the timekeeper there. Moor him to an ever fast mark. They remember that he'd smiled even as he leaked away. Laughing at his own great ill-fated feat. For he had fooled all of them. Perhaps even god. It was a grand joke. He had fooled everyone. Everyone but himself.

Norma Jean Howland

Hannah

He was afraid of crowds. Crowded places made his heart beat fast and hard, like it might break out of his chest. When the elevator doors closed Joshua stared at the floor, focusing on his scuffed shoes so he couldn't see the faces of the bodies pressing into him.

Joshua was a survivor. He had been in two concentration camps, Auschwitz and Buchenwald. Crowded into cattle cars and sleeping quarters. Standing in line for food, uniforms, and the number he wore on his arm. Watching silently as his mother and sister were taken away.

Once he had tried to run; he was a fast runner, but he couldn't outrun all the bullets. One came so close it burned a red mark across his cheek. When he could run no more, they beat him. He could only recall bits and pieces of those hours and the rest was a blank. He didn't try to escape again.

After that, Joshua made himself scarce, finding places to disappear in and tall men to stand behind. If they couldn't single him out maybe he wouldn't be beaten or shot. Of course he couldn't be sure, the rules weren't exactly clear. But it was his only hope, to go unnoticed.

He could still hear his sister crying as they were separated. Her shrill cries echoed in his ears, like a persistent ringing that would not stop. He should have saved her. He could have grabbed the Nazi's gun and freed the entire camp. His family and others could have escaped and Joshua would be a hero. But he had done nothing. Joshua had to face it, he was a coward.

Sometimes all he could do was put his hands over his ears to block out her cries.

He had one friend, a little boy named Abe. They found hiding places together and slept near each other, whispering into the night. But Abe caught a fever and died. After that, Joshua stayed close to his father. His father told him things he should remember. He wanted Joshua to have information, dates and places and addresses of relatives in America. Joshua tried to listen, but while his father talked, his mind wandered. Joshua couldn't seem to remember any of it. For some reason his father didn't know that along with being a coward, Joshua had become stupid.

The lights blinked and the elevator started to climb. Joshua felt his stomach heave and silently cursed his rotten belly.

In the camps his father had forced him to eat. Giving his own meager portion to his son. "Eat, eat," his father said, as he himself got sicker and could no longer stomach food. So Joshua went through the motions, choking down his father's food. It lay in his stomach like a rock. His father did not make it out of the camp. The day he died Joshua promised him he would make it to freedom. He had kept his promise.

On liberation day the soldiers were kind but they carried guns and Joshua didn't trust them. They were taken to a different camp. It was cleaner and there was more food. They told him he was free. Free to come to America. Joshua didn't know what else to do.

He had trouble sleeping. He lay awake listening to the camp sounds. Moans, snores and muted sobs. When he finally slept, nightmares chased him. Joshua watched as his family was herded over a cliff into a ravine. Down below were bodies, rotting flesh surrounded by flies. The smell was overpowering. He tried to save them, but he was always too late. He watched helplessly as they were pushed over the edge.

When he woke up, his heart would be pounding in his head like a hammer. He would fumble under his cot, reaching for the picture. Only when he had it would he be able to breathe normally again.

The photo had been taken in front of their house. His mother was young and his sister just a baby. He stared at the little boy; he didn't look familiar; Joshua didn't recognize him. His father looked healthy and strong. A man with a family and a future, nothing to fear.

Joshua made the journey to America, settling in New York City. There were relatives there. They gave him shelter and found him a job. They worried about him, he was so quiet and his eyes too sad for such a young man. They tried to ease his pain.

The fan in the elevator made a buzzing noise and stopped. A man behind him coughed. The sweat trickled down Joshua's neck, wetting his shirt.

Joshua got a job in a factory and worked hard but he didn't much like the city. It was too crowded and noisy. He found himself going to the library. He liked the quiet there. Although he couldn't read English, he found books with pictures. He walked up and down the rows of books, touching their worn bindings, thinking of his father. His father had loved to read. Joshua found books with pictures and maps of America. He was amazed at the size of this country.

He worked hard at his English, but his accent forced him to repeat most of his sentences. He spoke haltingly and his face reddened when he couldn't remember a word.

Joshua met a girl at the library. Her name was Rose. She smiled easily and had the whitest teeth Joshua had ever seen. She didn't seem to mind that he was so serious. She showed him New York. They went to the Statue of Liberty, Central Park and on a boat ride around New York Harbor. They went to movies and afterwards they walked. At night the city was quieter and not so crowded. They would walk for hours.

Rose loved Joshua from the start. She loved the way he walked, as if he didn't want to make a sound. She looked into his big eyes and wanted to take away the sadness. Swallow it whole.

The sweat soaked into his clothing. Little rivers forced their way into the small of his back. Joshua reached for his handkerchief but couldn't manage it without knocking into the old lady next to him. He licked the sweat off his lips. The perfume in the air was thick. In front of him a woman wore a large white hat with cherries on it. Joshua was so thirsty he wanted to eat one.

Joshua had grown into a good-looking man. He was small but the years of forced labor had made him strong. His dark eyes and shock of black hair was the envy of his co-workers. They made jokes and called him "Romeo." Joshua didn't mind, but would not laugh at their jokes. He cared nothing for looks, one way or another.

On Fridays, when the paychecks were handed out, he stood in line. When it was his turn to sign, the secretary smiled at him. When she gave him his pay her hand rested on his. Slightly stroking him with her blood red nails. Once she slipped a paper inside his envelope with her name and number on it. Her name was Marlene. He looked forward to Fridays so he could pretend not to notice her.

One Friday as he packed up his things, Marlene opened the door to the men's locker room and came in, locking it behind her. She was not a beautiful girl. She had large flat features, like the girls in the old country. Her body was plump and the nail polish looked out of place on her stubby fingers. She took off her dress and Joshua stood very still, afraid she would stop. He let himself go to her, lost in her cheap perfume; he forgot about everything.

The elevator lurched and the lady with the hat fell against him, stepping on his foot. A deep pain shot up his leg. She turned and whispered "Sorry." Her hair fell about her face in wisps and she towered over him. Before she turned around she winked at him. For a brief second he let himself think about burying his face in her hair.

Women were too friendly in America. They smiled at Joshua on trains and flirted with him on line at the bank. He would blush and stare at his shoes, but that made them try even harder. He didn't think he would ever understand these women. Sometimes when a girl smiled at him he found his eyes wandering over her body. One time he completely forgot to look at his shoes and reached over to touch her dress. He had never seen such a dress before. It was deep purple with little flowers on it and it felt like silk between his fingers. He could still feel the sharpness of her slap, the sting of it.

But Rose was different. Rose had asked him only once about the camps and his family. He showed her the photograph but there were things he kept to himself.

How could he explain to her the things he had seen? Tell her that once or twice a night he woke up with shivers. His whole body would shake like mad and all he could do was wait, wrapping himself tightly in the sheets until it stopped.

Rose was too good for him. He had seen what happens when human beings are reduced to animals. And he had done things he could never tell anyone. When you have lived in the face of evil there is no telling. He had grown a shell over his skin and he was hard. Mostly he lived in fear Rose would find out he was a coward.

Sometimes Joshua sat down to lunch and when he opened his paper bag he could smell the burning flesh again. On those days he would throw his lunch in the garbage.

He told Rose to forget about the past. He was an ordinary man and he had survived. That was all. Rose cried and kissed him on the cheek. Joshua held her, but not too close. He was afraid he might crush her.

They saw each other every day after work. On weekends she would invite him over for dinner. Her parents tried to like him but he was awkward, they didn't know how to make him at ease. Rose's mother was a good cook but Joshua's bad stomach prevented him from eating her delicious American cooking.

They were a working class family, living in Brooklyn. Rose was an only child and Joshua sensed they wanted something better for their daughter. Something other than an orphan who couldn't smile and rarely spoke. They had trouble seeing why Rose loved him, but they knew she did. They knew he was a kind of miracle and in time they accepted him.

The elevator came to a stop and the lights dimmed and went out. When they flickered back on, the doors slowly opened. Joshua went to the desk and stammered "Excuse me. I look for my wife. Rose Feldman."

The nurse looked at him over her glasses. "Room 312. It's down the hall to the left."

Joshua walked down the corridor shaking his head. Trying desperately not to run. When he saw Room 312 he stood outside the door. He was short of breath and he rocked back and forth slowly from side to side, front to back.

Finally he opened the door. He saw Rose and she smiled. The whiteness of her teeth blinded him so that all he could see was a brilliant light. He heard Rose calling him from a great distance but didn't know where she was. She sounded far away. "Joshua?"

Then he fell to earth. He was trembling and when he saw her he cupped Rose's face in his hands. They stood there like that for a time. When she spoke he jumped.

"Joshua, what should we name her?"

"I don't know. Maybe...maybe Hannah. My mother's name. Is it all right?"

"Hannah. I like it. Hello Hannah."

He looked down at the baby and she grabbed onto his finger. He was amazed at how tightly she held on. He put his face close to hers. He was afraid for her. He could never keep her safe.

But she squeezed his finger again and he felt how strong she was. As he looked down into her face, Joshua felt something inside him crack wide open. He smiled and whispered, “Hello Hannah.”

Annick Baud

✷

Blue-Eyed Friend from Far Away

Mother sewed a really pretty bathing suit for me, a two-piece bikini suit. I got to choose the material, with tiny yellow and white checkers. I designed it too, with a ruffled mini-skirt running around the waist. It had a bra, the first one I ever wore, even though I only had two tiny little nuts to cover. I loved my bathing suit. I felt so pretty in it.

Mother had gotten a secretarial job in Cannes, on the building site of a big, luxurious apartment complex erected right on the beachfront. These apartments were sold to millionaires, she told me. In her eyes, I saw the sadness: once a millionaire herself, she had recently tumbled through the maze of a painful separation from my father, forced to become an insignificant secretary, now working on a project for millionaires....

While she worked, I played on the beach, parading my beautiful bathing suit. It got lonely on the hot sand, though. Nobody ever talked to me. Wishing for a playmate, I ran after my own shadow along the shallow water's edge; I built sand palaces that were slowly erased by the gentle rhythm of the waves. Early in the morning, I found seashells washed upon the beach during the night, and I collected them. It was like finding treasures.

There was an ice-cream vendor on the boardwalk. I often lingered by his cart, but Mother never indulged in buying ice-cream, and I stopped asking for one. At lunchtime, all the workers poured out on the beach and sat in little groups to eat their sandwiches. Mother got her lunch break too, but much later, when all the men had already gone back to work.

One day, he came out of the dusty, clunky skeleton of the building site, all by himself. He didn't join any group, but sat alone by the water, facing the horizon at the far edge of the sea. He looked even lonelier than me. As if attracted by a magnet, I approached him, slowly imprinting in the sand a wide half moon of footsteps around him. He reminded me of the mighty Pharaoh standing on our dinning room buffet. I recognized the same noble features, with high cheekbones and elegant nose. As I was about to walk another half moon around him, he turned his majestic head and fixed his gaze on me. His eyes were blue, bright and deep like sparkling sapphires, a shade of color I had never seen before, tinged with purple. It stopped me in my tracks, right there by his side. He smiled. The infinite kindness and sadness in his smile instantly resonated with everything already stored in my own heart. I held my breath.

"The sea is so beautiful!" he said.

So, I sat next to him, both of us looking at the horizon on the far edge of the sea.

"I come from over the sea," he said, "way over there! From mountains standing tall on the other side of the sea."

Did he come from the same country as the Pharaoh? Maybe they were related.... So much longing in his voice....

"Do you miss it?" I asked.

"All day, all night, and every day..." he whispered, his shoulders suddenly sagging under an invisible, but heavy burden. "I have a little daughter just like you, over there," he added. "I miss her so much."

He looked at me again, telling me how they loved to play together. My father had played with me only once in my life, so I knew the man's longing. Reading the empathy in my eyes, he smiled softly and got up. In a few long and graceful strides, he reached the ice-cream cart and soon came back with an ice-cream cone in his hand.

"Here, this is what I would have given my daughter, if she was here. Please, take it on her behalf."

We sat in silence, looking at his country in the far distance, like two old friends. His little daughter's love for him was right there inside my heart, palpitating like a migrating bird, flying south ever so swiftly toward his country.

And then I heard my name being called. Mother was calling me from behind us. Her tone of voice didn't sound good at all.

"You better go," he said. I wanted to stay, though.

"We'll meet again?" I asked, knowing intrinsically that something precious was about to be lost.

"Maybe..." he murmured.

Still holding the end of my ice-cream cone, I reached Mother, who stood by her office door.

"What is this?" she asked suspiciously, pointing at the ice-cream cone.

"This nice man over there bought it for me as a present!" I exclaimed.

"You are NOT to accept anything from anybody you do not know, you hear me?" Mother hissed, hardly able to contain her anger and anxiety.

However she worded it, her message reached my mind like twisted poison-ivy tentacles: Arabs are not good people. "But, Mother, he's my friend!" Arabs cannot be trusted. "But, Mother, he has the clearest blue eyes I've ever seen!" Arabs are inferior to us. "But, Mother, he comes from the same land as the Pharaoh!"

"I never want you to talk to him again, you hear me? Never!" she said with such finality that tears came to my eyes. I looked where the man had been seated: his space was empty.

Next day, I saw him walking to the water's edge, but my feet stayed rooted on the boardwalk. Mother was all I really had in this world. How could I go against her wish, without betraying her? How could I not go to him, without betraying our friendship? My heart's ambivalence weighted me down, stealing away the impetus to run to him, to sit by his side and watch his far-away country on the distant horizon.

Like a bottled message thrown into the sea, I send this to you, over the years: beyond all the human prejudices that may turn our hearts into wastelands, we are friends in spirit. I know that you know that I will always love you.

Contributors

Born and raised in France, **Annick Baud** has lived in the U.S. for the last thirty years, where she is a painter, writer, Yoga instructor, and Reiki practitioner. "Blue-Eyed Friend..." was inspired by September 11th's tragedy. "Its aim is to remind every one of us what a child can do: to look at another human being through the many wrappings of color, role, and social status, and see the very core, the spirit within, the common element that makes us all One. If we, as so-called adults, truly looked at each other this way, our world would be a peaceful one."

Peter Cooper is the author of the novel, *Birthmark* (with Bill Rowe), and the poetry collection, *The Valley of My Western Heart*, both from Vivisphere Publishing. He lives in Stone Ridge. Other of his works can be seen at www.petercoop.com.

Wendy T. Dompieri returned to school and to writing after a thirty-year lull. The lull was not quiet. It was filled with people, relationships, and travel. Now, these life and travel experiences are used as backdrops in her work. Ms. Dompieri lives in Kingston and is presently working on her first screenplay.

Lanette Fisher-Hertz, a former non-profit executive and tabloid copy editor, is now teaching, writing, and pursuing her love of literature full-time thanks to the support of her reporter-husband of thirteen years, Larry Fisher-Hertz, and their two literary children. Her short story "Countdown" will appear in the third edition of *Women: Images and Realities, A Multicultural Anthology*.

Lucy Hayden is a writer of fiction and nonfiction, including profiles, essays, and reportage. Her story "Isolation" was recently published in the collection *I Thought My Father Was God* (Henry Holt, 2001). She lives and works in the Hudson Valley.

Norma Jean Howland was born on a farm near Spokane, Washington. She spent many years working in the theatre in NYC as both an actress and a writer. She received a NYSCA grant for her one-woman-show "Whore on a Cross" from Franklin Furnace. "Hannah" is based on her father-in-law's experiences in the concentration camps, and is dedicated to him.

Wendy Klein lives in Woodstock with her husband Brent Robison and is a full-time maskmaker and sculptor. What fascinates her most about writing stories is using language to create a three-dimensional world, like sculpting with words. "The Bus" was inspired by no one in particular on a cold and dreary carless day in December.

Dakota Lane is the author of the young adult novel *Johnny Voodoo* (Delacort) and has published short fiction in several anthologies. She is a freelance journalist living in Phoenicia.

Phillip P Levine calls himself a "poet, approximate". He is a two-year alumnus of Chenango Valley Writer's Conference and is a featured reader there. Phillip competed in the 2000 National Poetry Slam, and hosts a weekly open-mic in Woodstock. He recently performed on stage as Austin in Sam Shepherd's *True West* and is currently working on his first book of poetry, on a "poetry game," and on a one-person show tentatively titled, "5yrs. = 90mins." Phillip believes that our most desperate endeavor is to put meaning into our lives, and he does that by writing. "Soon" was written in the morning, when anything is possible.

H. N. Levitt has had Off-Broadway productions of his plays, most recently in 1998 at The Sage Theatre on West 42nd Street; an epic poem, *Achilles' Memoirs*, published by The Mellen Poetry Press, also in 1998; and short stories in various venues. The form and spirit of this story, "Incident at The Summer Writers' Conference," were influenced by Joyce's "Ivy Day in the Committee Room."

Iris Litt is the author of a book of poetry, *Word Love*, from Cosmic Trend Publications. She has had fiction, poems, essays and articles published in many magazines. Recent short story publications include *Travelers Tales, Out of the Catskills, The Second "Word Thursdays" Anthology, Cronos, Kaleidoscope*, and a first prize in the Virtual Press short story contest. She lives in Woodstock, where she leads writing workshops in fiction and poetry, and has taught at Ulster County Community College, Educational Alliance, New York Public Library, and others. Her time spent in Mexico has inspired stories and poems, including "The Stuff."

Jennie Litt's fiction and essays have appeared in The Sun, Indiana Review, Columbia, The Blue Moon Review, Speak, and Fireweed. Her full-length play, *Epiphany*, was produced at Circle Repertory Company (NYC) and the American Repertory Theater (Cambridge, MA), and published by Avon. She is currently at work on a novel, *Room Piece I*, an excerpt from which won the 2000 Mary Roberts Rinehart Award in fiction. She lives in Stone Ridge and Brooklyn, and moonlights as a cabaret singer.

Del Marbrook, a retired newspaper editor, is the author of the e-books *Alice Miller's Room* at OnlineOriginals and *Later For You* at DeadEndStreet. He recently finished a novel, *The Gold Factory*, about people who become the "prima materia" of a medieval alchemical manuscript. "Ice Storm, 1999" was inspired by sand sculptures found at Salvo on Cape Hatteras.

Philip Pardi is currently a Writing Fellow at the Michener Center for Writers. He has published poems most recently in *Borderlands*. He and his wife built their own home in the Catskills.

Fred Poole lives in Woodstock, where he leads the Authentic Writing workshops along with his wife, the writer Marta Szabo. Much of his published work has been set in the Far East, as in his Thailand novel *Where Dragons Dwell* and the exposé *Revolution in the Philippines*. But now, he says, he is finding even more intriguing material in the New England WASP worlds he knew in adolescence.

David Malcolm Rose is a sculptor currently living in Tennessee. "I was born and raised in the Catskill Mountains, as was my father and his father and so on back into the 1600s. Jacob Rose fought on both sides in the Revolution and, for his efforts, was hung behind the Senate House in Kingston. My great-grandfather was an itinerant stone cutter working the bluestone quarries around Woodstock. My grandfather was a subsistence farmer, part-time barber and blacksmith. My father was, and still is, a builder. I was a teenager when we scrapped the wood furnace for an oil burner. We have cut down a lot of trees in the Catskills."

Nicole Quinn has written for Egg Pictures, Showtime, HBO, and network television. She is a member of Actors & Writers in Olivebridge, and lives in Accord.

Brent Robison makes his living as a multimedia writer/producer. He won a 1995-96 Fiction Writers Fellowship from the New Jersey Council on the Arts, and has published short stories in *re:Issue*, *Alchemy*, and *Crania*. An '80s immigrant to the NYC area from Utah, he followed love north to the Catskills, and now lives with his wife Wendy Klein on the far western border of Woodstock.

Jessica Schabtach is a writer and editor who lives in Woodstock. Born in Oregon, she has been a social worker in West Virginia, a milliner in New Orleans, and a textbook editor in New York City. She is the author of an unpublished short novel, *American Cities*.

One day **Kate Schapira** will run a small press and make good writing cheaply available to everyone. One day her grant to teach writing and history in prison will come through. One day someone will publish another story of hers, but "All Saints" is the first one so far. In the meantime, she lives in Germantown, writes like a madwoman, and moonlights as an international jewel thief.

Nina Shengold won the ABC Playwright Award for *Homesteaders* and the Writers Guild Award for *Labor of Love*, starring Marcia Gay Harden. Her teleplays include *Blind Spot*, starring Joanne Woodward and Laura Linney, *Unwed Father* and *Double Platinum*; she adapted Jane Smiley's *Good Will* for American Playhouse. Ms. Shengold has edited seven theatre anthologies for Viking Penguin and Vintage Books, and is Artistic Director of Actors & Writers, a theatre company based in Olivebridge, NY. She has lived in the Hudson Valley since 1988 and is currently writing a novel.

Marilyn Stablein's *The Census Taker: Tales of a Traveler in India and Nepal* won a Seattle King County award and a Houston Brazos award. Other books include: *Vermin: A Bestiary; Night Travels to Tibet*; and *Climate of Extremes: Landscape and Imagination*. She is also a visual and performance artist. Recent collaborations include: Bardo Passages: Soul Journeys to Tibet; Himalayan Travelogues and Sacred Waters. She is co-director of Alternative Books in Kingston and a founder of the Hudson Valley Publishing Network.

Marta Szabo lives in Woodstock with her husband, Fred Poole. Together they offer the Authentic Writing workshops, which Fred founded almost ten years ago. Marta has been pursuing the mystery of writing since being a teenager in her attic bedroom where she read without stopping and listened to the radio and waited to leave home and have adventures. She recently received an MFA in Creative Writing from Goddard College and is writing the stories of her life adventures so far, especially the most dastardly ones. She likes writing that shouts out in places where silence has been imposed.

Valerie Wacks is a real estate attorney in Ulster County. Her poetry has been published in *the Subterraneans*, *Voices of Selene, Echoes of Avalon*, and *In Country*. She is currently revising her second novel whilst her first novel wanders forlorn in search of a publisher.